1920

DIPS INTO
THE NEAR FUTURE

An Anti-War
Pamphlet from World War I

By

J. A. HOBSON

First published in 1917

British Library Cataloguing-in-Publication Data
A catalogue record for this book is available
from the British Library

CONTENTS

WORLD WAR ONE

The First World War was a global war centred in Europe that began on 28 July 1914 and lasted until 11 November 1918. More than nine million combatants were killed, a casualty rate exacerbated by the belligerents' technological and industrial sophistication – and tactical stalemate. It was one of the deadliest conflicts in history, paving the way for major political changes, including revolutions in many of the nations involved. The war drew in all the world's economic great powers, which were assembled in two opposing alliances: the Allies (based on the Triple Entente of the United Kingdom, France and the Russian Empire) and the Central Powers of Germany and Austria-Hungary. These alliances were both reorganised and expanded as more nations entered the war: Italy, Japan and the United States joined the Allies, and the Ottoman Empire and Bulgaria joined the Central Powers. Ultimately, more than 70 million military personnel were mobilised.

The war was triggered by the assassination of Archduke Franz Ferdinand of Austria, heir to the throne of Austria-Hungary, by a Yugoslav nationalist, Gavrilo Princip in Sarajevo, June 28th 1914. This set off a diplomatic crisis when Austria-Hungary delivered an ultimatum to Serbia, and international alliances were invoked. Within weeks, the major powers were at war and the conflict soon spread around the world. By the end of the war, four major imperial powers; the German, Russian, Austro-Hungarian and Ottoman empires—ceased to exist. The map of Europe was redrawn, with several independent nations restored or created. On peace, the League of Nations formed with the aim of preventing any repetition of such an appalling conflict, encouraging cooperation and communication between the newly autonomous nation states. This laudatory pursuit failed spectacularly with the advent of the Second World War however, with new European nationalism and the rise of fascism paving the way for the next global crisis.

This book is part of the World War One Centenary series; creating, collating and reprinting new and old works of poetry, fiction, autobiography and analysis. The series forms a commemorative tribute to mark the passing of one of the world's bloodiest wars, offering new perspectives on this tragic yet fascinating period of human history.

PREFACE

NOW that Dora's claws are clipped it may be safe for me to admit that these dialogues were intended not as a prophecy of 1920, but as a mocking revelation of the folly and malignity of the Never-Endian attitude of 1917. Satire seemed the only means of exposing a mind of bottomless credulity, never weary of denouncing the wickedness of its enemy and acclaiming its own virtues; betraying every cause of liberty at home in a war of liberty; boastful of its own modesty and moderation, while openly competing with the enemy barbarities of word and deed; claiming to end war by refusing every opportunity of making peace; and, finally, exhibiting a really genuine indignation that any of these charges of inconsistency should be brought against it.

Satire, aiming at self-recognition, naturally works by a selection and exaggeration, and the method here adopted consisted in the creation of a fictitious "1920," so that the facts of 1917 might by a plausible process of growth, assume shapes so monstrous that their folly and their dangers could no longer escape detection. It seems necessary to give this explanation, because more than one of my critics have seriously complained of the distorted and unfair selection of topics in my treatment, objecting that I had neglected to hold the balance fair between the Never-Endians and the Pacifist, and had ignored the crimes and follies of the enemy, a line of criticism which has a humour of its own.

It is likely, therefore, that persons may be found capable of saying that because peace has been made on terms which will make 1920 other than it is here depicted, the argument of my satire has already been refuted. I must, therefore, repeat that my game was 1917, not 1920. But I may add that, if the disappointed

Never-Endians in this country and our Allies work their will, the militarism crushed in Germany will break out in the demand for a new Holy Alliance to secure social order in each allied country and to impose "good government" upon the rest of Europe. The task of maintaining a world just dangerous enough to furnish a pretext for retaining conscription and the class rule it involves, but not so dangerous as gravely to imperil property, contains a separate challenge to the comic spirit. Dora, though subdued in her activities, is by no means dead; the new arts of manufacture of war-truth offer limitless possibilities of application to peace-truth; and intestine disorders, stimulated by tactful mismanagement, may form a tolerable substitute for war itself. So Cheer up, Never-Endians! All is not yet lost.

LUCIAN.
December, 1918.

1920
DIPS INTO
THE NEAR FUTURE

BY LUCIAN [1]

[1] The pseudonym of John A. Hobson, a reference to Lucian of Samosata, a first century Assyrian satirist.

CHAPTER I

THE AGED SERVICE ACT

I HAD been up country for the last two years opening up new stations for the Inland Mission, [1] and rarely meeting any European during the whole time. Letters and papers took anything from three to six months to reach me, so that when I determined to come home and just caught the boat at Hong Kong, I probably knew less of the recent happenings of the war than any other white man in the world. [2] Mixing freely with the few other passengers on board, I naturally picked up what I could, but the latest cables of the exciting events upon the Western Front, [3] together with the *personalia* [4] of the war, crowded out the interest of the internal situation of England. I knew that the George Government [5] had long fallen, and I gathered that the nation was feeling the pinch of food shortage more sharply than before, but otherwise had little preparation for the state of things that confronted me when the express from Plymouth landed me in London late one night in May, and a needed night's rest set me free to rediscover my native land.

[1] The China Inland Mission, a Protestant missionary society.

[2] The Great War, or "the war to end all wars," or World War I as it later came to be known, began militarily in mid 1914.

[3] The German army had invaded Luxembourg and Belgium, then gained control of part of France. The line of invasion and defense, known as the Western Front, ran more or less diagonally from the northwest to the southeast, with the Allies – eventually England, France, etc. – on the (South) West side and the Central Powers –

11

Germany, etc. – on the (North) East.

[4] Anecdotes about people.

[5] David Lloyd George (born 1863) had become Prime Minister of England December 1916.

As I stepped out of Morley's Hotel [1] my attention was at once caught by a long, black-coated procession making for Parliament Street. It was headed by a figure I recognised at once as the aged Bishop of Silchester, who had ordained me six years ago. There followed in a rude four-formation a seemingly endless array of white or grey-haired men and women of every social grade, some marching upright and alert, others bowed, depressed, and slouching, as if bent on some unwilling errand which yet they were unable to refuse. Right in the foremost group, to my surprise, I recognised two figures with which the illustrated Press had made me familiar as members of the recently deposed Government. As I was gazing, who should pass but young Priestley, whom I had not seen since leaving Oxford, but he spotted me at once, and greeted me in his usual cheery fashion. After a brief interchange of personalities, I asked him what this solemn procession was about.

[1] An oblique reference to John Morley, member of the House of Lords, who had opposed England's declaration of war against Germany. In his "Memorandum on Resignation" he said that most of the Cabinet had decided to declare war on Germany before it had invaded Belgium.

"What, my dear Charteris!" he exclaimed, "don't you really know? To-day is the fortnightly dedicatory service at the Abbey."

"Dedicatory service," I said. "Why, what do you mean?"

"But is it possible," he replied, "that you haven't heard? Why, to-day is the day of Supreme Sacrifice, and this is the ceremonial march of victims."

"Sacrifice! Victims!" I repeated, and then the wild thought

struck me of something I had read in a speculative writer on psychology, about the possibility of a collective throwback to atavistic standards under some powerful emotional stress. Is this a return to Druidism? [1]

[1] The Druids were the priests of the ancient Celtic societies which once existed throughout much of the British Isles and Western Europe north of the Alps. They left no written record and little is known about them. That they practiced human sacrifice may have been Roman propaganda.

At last Priestley really understood how ignorant I was of what had taken place in the last few months, and set about explaining things. He first told me how, since the official food-fakers (that was his rude word) [1] had cancelled "the law of supply and demand" last summer, things had drifted steadily from bad to worse. Bad harvests and short transport inevitably shortened supplies, while the fixing of low prices stimulated demand. This was "asking for trouble." Hidden for several months by the usual official methods, the vision of the wolf at the door was suddenly revealed to the public eye in January by an offended editor, and the starvation-panic swelled to storm-point with startling rapidity. No Government could possibly stand against it, and the George contraption went down like a rickety gate. "Stop food-waste, and save the war!" became the universal slogan, and the Northcliffe Press, [2] assisted by the *Morning Post* and *John Bull*, soon hoisted into the saddle a choice selection of "the younger statesmen" to enforce food economy. There was only one course open. All idle talk of ploughing up the parks and of compulsory labour on allotments was dropped in favour of the single drastic policy of husbanding our dwindling food supply for the sole use of our fighting forces and our industrial effectives engaged in necessary national services.

[1] Soon after entering the war the British government enforced the

sale of light bread and other "watered down" basic foodstuffs.

[2] The Northcliffe Press was one of the many newspapers, including the *Times*, owned by Lord Northcliffe (Alfred Harmsworth), who used them to promote his political views.

There was a moment when the extreme demands of the Food Control seemed to threaten child-life as well as old age. The whole available food should be reserved for those who were helping to win the war. But the children were saved by critics pointing out the overwhelming case in favour of a long duration for the war and the necessity of universal military service afterwards. To starve our children now would be bad military economy, for they would be wanted as cannon-food later on.

"And so," he explained, "it soon came to be recognised that, if food consumption was to be diminished appreciably, the old people must be sacrificed. In point of fact, they were not worth their keep."

"But," I broke in, "was there no sense of reverence, no rally of national affection to stop this terrible resolve?"

"Yes," he replied; "of course, it caused a great deal of heart-searching. Indeed, it was not till the new Archbishop (one of the youngest to attain this high office) had shown in an impressive sermon at St. Paul's (a sermon circulated over the whole country by the Supreme Sacrifice Committee) how Christianity had always recognised and incorporated the best tenets and the noblest practices of the Stoic philosophy, that the educated classes came to acquiesce in the necessity of the new proposal. The bitterest resentment, curiously enough, was manifested among the poorest classes, who clung to their old and feeble with a really obstinate ferocity. It was not the least use explaining to them the urgent necessity of State or the glory of the Supreme Sacrifice. Yes; there were really terrible scenes. The rich, be it said to their credit, gave up their old folk much more patriotically than the poor. Traitorous pro-Germans, who sought to crab the scheme, used to hint that inheritance, even with the present high

Death Duties, was a considerable consolation. But this, of course, was mere malice.

"No! What really won the day for the Supreme Sacrifice was the sheer logic of the situation. It was best set out in the new Government's reasoned poster:' To save defeat the nation must eat less; soldiers and workers cannot eat less; therefore, the aged and the idlers must not eat!'"

"And so," said I, "it has come to this glorious band of martyrs cheerfully surrendering their lives at the call of King and Country."

Priestly glanced at me curiously. "Well," he said, "yes, if you like to put it so. Yes, I admit they are putting the best face on it. But, you see, they have no option."

"You don't mean to say," I broke in, "that this is a forced national service, that these poor old men and women are driven like cattle into the State Crematorium!"

"Well," he replied, "you put it a little crudely. But the plain facts are these: The old men, who made speeches on recruiting platforms and sat on tribunals earlier in the war, had pitched the note of national duty and self-sacrifice so high when they were sending young men out into the trenches, and had lamented so loudly their own inability to risk their lives, that when the Younger Statesmen first framed their scheme, they launched it on a voluntary basis. They got the King, [1] personally, to approach three or four of the most enthusiastic' Never-Endians' [2] among the older peers and commoners, and to get a few bishops, heads of colleges, and patriotic editors to give' a friendly lead' in the voluntary sacrifice."

---

[1] George V.

[2] A derogatory term invented by opponents of the war who believed it would never end, applied to people who wanted to win it, that is, to subjugate Germany. By December 1916 Germany and the other Central Powers had offered England a *status quo ante bellum* peace, which the English government rejected as a war maneuver.

"You don't mean to say the King failed again?"

"Oh, yes! Voluntary service, as before, proved a complete fiasco! No more good for lives than for liquor. [1] Two or three of those approached appeared to dally with the proposal, but were won over by the tearful remonstrances of their relatives (so they said); most of them stonily refused, suggesting that the very existence of persons of their quality was a national service. Though they might not appear to be doing much, they were sustaining the spirit of the nation. Some of them even had the hardihood to put in a formal plea to this effect for exemption before the Tribunals."

[1] That is, voluntary service was no more effective than voluntary abstinence from drinking. See Part IV – D.O.R.A., second footnote to first paragraph.

"What Tribunals?" I asked.

"Oh! they were set up last February when the Aged Service Act was made compulsory. Only men of military age can sit on the Tribunals, for though only men over sixty-five at present come under the Act, it is recognised that it may be necessary later on to lower the exemption age; while, on the other hand, the Military Service Age may have to be raised. So it was felt safer at the outset to confine the *personnel* of these Tribunals to men of military age."

"But can these men, bearing no risks to themselves, be always relied upon to do justice to Conscientious Objectors or other claimants for exemption among the aged?"

"Well, I don't mind telling you that a good deal of trouble has arisen on this head. It was largely due to the drafting of the exemption clause. Late one night, near the end of the Session, a snap division in the Lords (there is a larger proportion of old men in regular attendance than in the Commons) slipped in a conscientious objection as a ground for exemption, and the Government, in order to save time and with their usual recklessness, let it pass. The consequence might, of course, have been foreseen. Lord H., with his legal acumen, at once pounced on the flaw, and helped to organize an Anti-Crematorium League of those who had a moral objection to die before their time. They even put up before the Tribunals the plea that, when an old man said he had a conscience, it devolved upon the representative of the Supreme Sacrifice Service to prove a negative. This, of course, was quickly brushed aside. More trouble was caused by bringing reputable witnesses of military age to support the statement of Objectors that they had always been known to hold the strange doctrine that every man had an indefeasible right to live out the full natural life, as defined by the Apostle Metchnikoff. [1] But the Younger Statesmen, with their secret orders to Tribunals, soon swept away this nonsense, and it was generally held that no aged man or woman actually had a conscience within the meaning of the Act, unless he or she was doing, or could show that he or she was capable of doing, certain specified forms of national work up to, or above, the standard of healthy middle-age. This regulation, however, was soon found to give too many loopholes of escape, and the growing pressure of food shortage in the stormy weeks of March aroused in the Northcliffe Press the' funk hole' [2] cry. Aged busybodies with some' pull' were found slipping through on the plea that the committees on which they sat for minding other peoples' business were national service. It was shown by convincing argument that in an age of strain and hustle, a bishop or a judge or a professor was no good after sixty-five, or that his work could either be dispensed with, or shared out among two or three younger men far more competent than he and eager for the opportunity.

<hr>

[1] Élie Metchnikoff (Ilya Ilyich Mechnikov 1845 – 1916) was a Russian (later French) microbial biologist famous for discovering that phagocytes (white blood cells) engulf harmful microbes, providing an innate immunity. He also held that aging is due

to toxic bacteria in the gut and that life could be prolonged by possessing the right sort of bacteria. In his book *The Prolongation of Life: Optimistic Studies* he uses the phrase "apostles of optimism" to mean people who persevere with good humor despite adversity.

[2] Generally a place of safe retreat, in war a foxhole or dugout, but here used derisively: a place to sit out the war in relative comfort.

"At first there was an attempt to apply the Aged Service Act only to unoccupied or retired persons over sixty-five years. But the Supreme Sacrifice Committee soon complained that doddering directors who put in an hour's attendance at a meeting once a fortnight, occasional reviewers for the Press, and tradesmen who kept their name in the firm, were getting exemption before slack tribunals. The new regulations, requiring doctors' certificates for clean bills of health during the three last years, and proof of holidays not exceeding one month's absence per annum, soon brought to book the senile shirker.

"But next, egged on by the same Press, our food economists made further claims. Not satisfied with saving the rations of several million aged folk, they began to turn their attention more closely to the German methods, and to cry out against what they called the crematory waste."

"Too horrible!" I exclaimed; "you mean the Kadaver-verwertungsanstalt! [1] But surely this abomination has been averted."

[1] Corpse Utilization Factory – for oil, soap and fertilizer – one of many (fabulous) atrocity stories of WW I. Perhaps here the author, though against the war, believed its promoters' propaganda.

"Indeed, I hope so," said my friend, "but the conflict between the economists and the humanitarians is still going on. The former insist that our straits admit of no squeamish sentimentalism. If it is degrading, the blame rests with the Huns, [1] who set the example, and forced us to follow. Unfortunately, they have just got support from an unexpected quarter, the bishop-designate to Silchester, whose letter to *The Times* puts in what Dodson (you remember Dodson) irreverently terms' the sacramental touch.' He even questions the propriety of using the term, ' supreme sacrifice, ' unless it is thus' consummated'—that is the phrase.

[1] Huns was a derogatory epithet for Germans. It alludes to the former Kaiser's exhortation to his troops before he sent them to China to help put down the Boxer rebellion. He told them to take no prisoners and become as infamous as the Huns of Attila. In other words, he asked for it. (England and Germany were allies during the Boxer rebellion, late 1899 to 1901.)

"Nay, there is some reason to fear that this combination of economists and sacramentalists will have their way, especially if they can rally the swell-mob [1] of the *Morning Bull* [2] with their bludgeon arguments, 'Don't you want to win the war? What does the fate of these fag-ends of humanity matter compared with the feeding of our brave lads in the trenches?'

[1] Swell mob, according to an old dictionary: "The better-dressed thieves and pickpockets."
[2] The magazine *John Bull*, the title referring to the personification of England, founded by Horatio Bottomley, a swindler, journalist and politician who promoted the war. See Horatio Bottomley.

"But the humanitarians have so far held their ground. So if you want to see the procession to Golder's Green [1] after the dedication service in the Abbey, you are just in time."

[1] Where is located a crematorium and mausoleum of the same name.

CHAPTER II

REPRISALS

PRIESTLY asked me to dine with him at his Club that evening. He would get Dodson, who happened to be working with him in Section 426 of the Food Control, which was housed in the warren underneath Hyde Park. He would also try to get Marlow—Marlow of "The House"—who was back on a few days' leave. He held a high command in the Air Service, and would be able to give us the latest from the only front that really counted.

Most of the morning and afternoon I spent in fathoming Underground London. As soon as the Air had definitely established its supremacy over land and sea, all well-to-do and official London set about burrowing for safety. The West End and the more prosperous suburbs had dug themselves in some time ago, their occupants only emerging when the bad-weather signal was hoisted. Beginning first with extensions and improvements of existing cellar accommodations, they soon set about sinking shafts and opening up lower stories, until the big hotels and appartment houses became veritable "Hell-scrapers." I was puzzled at first by the gigantic quantity of labour that must have been put into these structures. But the labour problem was really a simple one. Most of the grown-up inhabitants of the West End had long ago become Government officials. Their lives were no longer their own; the safety of the State demanded their personal security. It therefore naturally occurred to the National Service Control that there were a couple of million able-bodied men, once more or less skilled workmen in various trades, who by this time were good for nothing else but digging—the only

20

useful thing they had been taught to do since they were enlisted. Here they were scattered about Great Britain in camps, eating their heads off and growing stale for all war-purposes. Farmers had tried in vain to get their help in growing food for the nation. Providence had reserved them to save the West End of the Metropolis—the brain-centre of the Empire.

Hence the immensely rapid spread of subterranean officialism. But officials do not live in offices and their claim that official inviolability should be extended to their private residences was soon conceded. Officials above a certain rank were soon entitled to a draft of military diggers as a perquisite of office. Other well-to-do families were next allowed to hire a draft of labour as a source of war-finance. Districts, outside the brain and money areas, were, of course, unable to get adequate underground protection, and had been terribly reduced in population by the air-warfare. There was, I gathered, a good deal of ill-feeling manifested in what might now almost be termed open-air London, for so large a part of it was by this time roofless, its denizens crouching within their battered walls, or else camping permanently in the Tubes [1] now given up to them.

[1] Subway tunnels.

Priestley had been lucky in securing Marlow, and after we had descended to the new club dining-room, on the fifth floor, and handed each his sheaf of food-tickets to the head waiter, we settled down to a quite comfortable and even luxurious repast. Dodson insisted, half, I think, in earnest, that well-to-do officialism was able to "do itself" far better, and utilise more freely its various pulls and privileges, now that its subterranean life removed it from the vulgar gaze.

But Priestley was evidently anxious to draw Marlow on war prospects, and used my simplicity and curiosity as a pretext. Just before his leave, Marlow had had the honour of an interview with Sir Benjamin Lewis himself at headquarters. The Commander-in-Chief had expressed, he said, the utmost confidence in a successful decision within a reasonable time. The *moral* [1] of the enemy was visibly weakening. The nation had only to preserve a united front, and endure for a few more years. In my innocence, I broached a question as to the line upon the main Front and the chance of breaking through. Marlow stared at me with astonishment until Priestley told him my peculiar situation. He then remarked: "Breaking through! Bless me! You are back in prehistoric times." Sir Benjamin's confidence, it appears, had nothing to do with land operations. Trench paralysis was long ago, Marlow told me, an accepted fact. Sir Benjamin and all of them "looked higher" for their source of confidence. For a moment I imagined that Marlow was touched by some spiritual prompting—though that was not the Marlow I remembered. But he soon made it quite plain. Land and sea war were now "back numbers." The only really effective way of killing Germans was by air. The War Council was at last thoroughly convinced of this. "Why, when I was called in the other day to present my report at Downing Street [2] in person, 'Orace [3] said to me—" "Who is 'Orace?" I whispered to Priestley. He burst out laughing. "Don't you really know? I forgot. It must have taken place when you were at sea. It was, of course, a fierce struggle with Lord Northcliffe, who made sure of the succession. But 'Orace' with his' John Bull Clubs,' [4] downed him—denounced him up and down the country for laying out' A Yankee victory' " [5]

---

[1] *moral*: French for morale.

[2] The Prime Minister lives at 10 Downing Street, London.

[3] Horatio Bottomley, publisher of the magazine *John Bull* (see a previous footnote about him).

[4] There was a "John Bull Victory Bond Club," one of the most craven of Bottomley's investment frauds as it turned out later.

[5] The U.S. had entered the war in April 1917, which ensured an Allied victory. The satire of course is dated, the war ended September 1918, the Allies crushing Germany. U.S. entry, by the

way, was a disaster for America – it brought more fascism ("big government") to America. And a disaster for Europe – if the U.S. had stayed out of the war the Europeans would have reached an armistice ending the war earlier, staying out probably would have prevented the Russian Revolution (which occurred as these installments were being written), and the Allies, in the Treaty of Versailles, would not have been able to saddle Germany with the entire responsibility for the war, leaving Germans with grievances which Hitler exploited later, resulting in World War II. See The Disaster of America's Entry in The Great War.

I had by this time come to recognise that Marlow was a greater personage than I had thought. Every man who passed our table glanced at him with open admiration. At last Priestley began to chaff Marlow for his modesty, and explained to me how Marlow was the man who planned out the splendid bombing excursion to Leipsic [1] on Easter Day, when our air-force got above the German barrage and dropped several thousand bombs on the great school-children's procession—the most brilliant scoop of the year. "Why, yesterday he had conferred on him the new Order of the Star of Bethlehem." [2]

[1] The city of Leipzig, Germany, archaically spelled.
[2] A religious order. Their first location, Bishopsgate, became a mental hospital. The courtyard adjoining was Bedlam.

I whispered a word about "reprisals."

"Reprisals!" repeated Dodson. "Why, that foolish word is happily almost extinct. It belonged to the period of humanitarian humbug, when patriots still pretended to distinguish between big and little Huns, male and female Huns, innocent and guilty Huns. Now, thank heaven! we recognise only two sorts of Huns— live Huns and dead Huns."

"But surely," I broke in. "Why, I remember just before I left England, how General Smuts, [1] in that eloquent speech in which he sorrowfully admitted the necessity of reprisals, said: 'We shall use every endeavor to spare, as far as is humanly possible, the innocent and the defenceless.'"

[1] Jan Smuts. In 1917 he was Lieutenant-General. He recommended attacks on German civilians to destroy their morale. Germany attacked civilians too in its Zeppelin and aircraft raids on London.

"Yes, of course," rejoined Dodson; "but you must remember the governing principle of national duty to which a Liberal newspaper referred as "the hard logic of frightfulness." And then, as an ex-journalist, he began to dilate upon the yeoman's service rendered by the Press in soothing the qualms of the "sentimentalists," and in showing how a continued execration of Hun methods was quite consistent with imitation of them. Indeed, the newspapers gave the nation a most serviceable lead over the stile [1] by pointing out that we were entitled to hate the Hun in exact proportion to the moral turpitude of every method which he forced us to adopt!"

[1] Stile: a set of steps for passing over a fence or wall, here meant metaphorically.

"But," again I interrupted, "no nation can force another to degrade itself."

"I am sorry to seem rude," retorted Dodson, "but your crude ethics, plausible as they appeared at first, were soon disposed of by the *Westminster* [1] in a convincing judgment which I think I can remember:' We cannot give the enemy the military and moral advantage of practising on our nation what we do not practise on his'—a rendering of the Golden Rule, the equity and elevation of which at once commended themselves to all right-thinking people."

[1] The Westminster Gazette was an influential newspaper based

in London and at this time owned by Alfred Mond (see a later footnote about him).

The Churches, too, Priestley informed me, rallied gallantly round the spiritual emergency. Indeed, the last scruples of anti-patriotic sentimentalism were stifled by the famous vote of Convocation in favour of a "diluted Christianity," operating through the instrument of a National Indulgence to practise Mosaic morality for the duration of the war. This entailed some readjustment in the services. "Back to Moses!" became the spiritual slogan, and a drastic reconstruction of the Rubric removed from the Lessons of the Day the more enervating chapters of the Gospels, and gave due prominence to the bracing incidents in Joshua and Judges. [1] A general assent was readily accorded to the charge which the good Bishop of Porchester gave to his diocesan clergy: "Above all, remember that a genuinely Catholic Christianity must learn to adapt itself to the special character and peculiar spiritual requirements of every great occasion in the national life. Thus, and only thus, can it maintain its full potency as a living, an organic creed." And, again, he adds this inspiring apophthegm: [2] "It belongs to the wisdom of the serpent sometimes to lay aside the innocence of the dove."

[1] Rubric: here, the rule for conducting the church service. Joshua and Judges are books of the Old Testament telling of the Israelites' bloodthirsty battles.
[2] British variant of "apothegm."

Priestley, finding the conversation getting beyond his depth, recalled it to a more practical direction by alluding to the latest current controversy in the policy of air-war. It appears that air-strategy had gone through a long process of evolution in working out its "net economy." At first, the new air plans were mostly concentrated upon the great industrial centres, both here and in Germany. Lancashire and the West Riding, and the new munition towns, passed through a terrible time, until they had learned to bury their most vulnerable limbs. Though London's large poor areas still offered a serviceable practice-ground for half-trained German fliers seeking an easy prey, it soon seemed that the West-End enjoyed a fair immunity. Some put this down to the superior subterranean defences I have described. But others said there was evidence from captured German air-orders that the brain-centre was avoided by a calculated policy. The German militarists still wanted to win the war. Anyhow, the fact of this comparative immunity was undeniable. But, as time went on, strategy on both sides underwent a transformation. There was less and less concentration upon material objectives, and more attention was devoted to selection of human targets. Primarily, no doubt, it was a question of killing numbers, and chiefly by the explosion of infectives. But now that the aged and the feeble on both sides had been removed by the adoption of a more enlightened food economy, all sorts of the surviving population were rightly accounted belligerents. All sorts, however, were not of equal value. Everything depended here upon the estimated duration of the war. A short time-focus obviously gave most importance to the existing vigorous adult population. But those who took a longer range insisted that the true economy in killing Germans on the one side, British on the other, was to concentrate upon the rising generation. Yet even among the so-called "baby-killing" party a difference arose which gave rise to a most acrimonious controversy in the patriotic Press. Those who based their calculations on a further five or even ten years' war, urged that preferential treatment in the killing should be given to boys who were actually ripening into airmen, while those who gave a longer duration to the war insisted that the main effort should be directed against the future mothers of the race. This faction was called "the feminists." A very little reflection was needed to show how intricate were the convolutions of this controversy.

* * * * *

Just as our talk was drawing to a close, and we were about to rise from the table, who should pass along from a far corner of the room where he had been dining but Filmer of Exeter [1] —familiarly known in our Oxford set as the Early Christian, because of the regularity of his attendance at Morning Chapel, and his general piety. Priestley informed me that Filmer was evidently on leave from Dartmoor, where he had spent the last four years as a hardened C.O. [2] As he passed our table with a nod of recognition, Dodson called out in his rudest, public-schoolboy manner, "Hullo, Filmer! back again to Paganism? What price Christianity to-day?" "Same old price," was Filmer's quick reply. "Thirty pieces of silver."

[1] A college of Oxford University.
[2] Conscientious objectors were housed in Dartmoor Prison, Devonshire.

:

CHAPTER III

THE LABORATORY OF WAR-TRUTH

IN one of my early voyages of discovery amid the warrens of the war-bureaucracy I came upon Paston, whom I had left some years ago at Oxford, a young philosophy don, one of the brightest and most enthusiastic exponents of the Pragmatist gospel. [1] He explained to me that he had chucked the 'Varsity, and was engaged in war-work. Seeing me smile and guessing the cause (for Paston had been President of the Norman Angell Club), [2] he thought some explanation was desirable, and urged me to come into his "hut" and have a talk. I gladly accepted the invitation, for I was interested to learn what line of war-work could have attracted Paston.

[1] C. S. Peirce (1839-1914), an American philosopher, founded Pragmatism in the late 19th century, and two other American philosophers, William James (1842-1910) and especially John Dewey (1859-1952) elaborated it. John Dewey welcomed U.S. entry into the war as a way to destroy private property in America. See his article "What Are We Fighting For?" in *The Independent*, June 22, 1918, later reprinted as the chapter "The Social Possibilities of War" in *Characters and Events* – social as in socialism.

[2] British economist Norman Angell (1872-1967) in 1909 had written the anti-war pamphlet *Europe's Optical Illusion* and in 1910 the book *The Great Illusion* subtitled *A Study of the Relation of Military Power in Nations to Their Economic and Social Advantage*. The title for the 1937 French film *La Grande Illusion* was taken from the title of Angell's book.

Pretending to be surprised at my surprise, he spun out a quite convincing story. "Why, the war brought me the chance of a hundred life-times. I might have spent all the remainder of my days grinding out futile plausibilities in that fusty old place without ever discovering the glorious significance of Pragmatism, if it hadn't been for the war."

"But what," I interjected, "can the war have to do with Pragmatism?"

"Why, just everything," he replied. "Of course, I remember you didn't take' Greats,' [1] but you must have gathered in a general way what Pragmatism means."

¹ The Philosophy and Ancient Languages course at Oxford.

"Why, yes," I replied, "I gathered that you Pragmatists held that the actual world of experience was a sort of jelly on which a man stamped his own meaning and personal purposes, and that the truth of any statement depended on whether' it worked.'"

"Yes," he broke in, "you've got the guts of the idea quite right. Truth is what works. But works for what? The one weak spot in pre-war Pragmatism was its failure to give a really convincing answer to this question. With a sudden flash of illumination, war, the intensest of all human purposes, brought the needed answer. Truth is what helps to win the war. Directly I realised the supreme significance of this judgment, I saw also how famously it fitted on to that political philosophy of State Absolutism, which came to us from Hobbes, [1] not from the charlatan Hegel, [2] as the men of Balliol [3] so falsely taught. I had discovered what Pragmatism was really' for.' I felt myself a man with a mission, and immediately offered to put at the disposal of the Government a general scheme for the production and distribution of war-truth, substituting a really scientific method for the clumsy empiricism of their censorship and war-news department."

[1] Thomas Hobbes, 17th century English philosopher famous for the book *Leviathan*, which argued in favor of absolute monarchy as a "social contract" among formerly equal individuals. Once in place the sovereign is all-powerful and can do no wrong. The original frontpiece of *Leviathan* depicted a crowned giant striding the earth and a quote from Job in Latin, the translation: "There is no power on earth to be compared with him."

[2] Georg Wilhelm Friedrich Hegel (1770 – 1831), German philosopher who advocated worship of the State whereby one finds "real freedom."

[3] Balliol, among the oldest colleges of Oxford. One of its Masters in the late 19th century was Edward Caird, an influential promoter of Hegel.

"Well, I gather that they took you on, though I must say the project seems on first view to have an uncommonly German look. They have made you manager of a sort of Wahrheits-Fabrik, [1] I suppose from the large-lettered inscription over your door, 'Psychological Laboratory for the Preparation of War-Truth.' I must confess that your whole conception of war-truth is a little disturbing to an old-fashioned fogey like myself."

[1] Truth-Factory.

"Well," Paston spoke a little warmly, "we are all put upon war-bread, why not upon war-truth? If you reflect, you will realise that the analogue is just and even necessary. As Emerson so beautifully expresses it, 'The laws above are sisters of the laws below.' It is, indeed, this philosophic harmony that gives validity to all our spiritual war-processes. This you would better understand, if I explain the fuller military service of which I am only a divisional commander."

"Well, go ahead," I replied, "it's all new to me, and I want to understand."

And then he launched into the whole story of the Conscription of the Mind. "Though quite early in the conflict we had pretended to regard it as a War of Ideas, it took several years before we were really prepared as a nation to mobilise upon this basis. We didn't see at first that in a War of Ideas the State must have complete control over the intellectual and moral resources of the nation. So for some years we went fumbling on with departmental Censorships, continually overlapping or tripping one another up, and allowing all sorts of damaging talk and writing to go on because of foolish distinctions made in Parliament between suppression of news and suppression of opinion. A Pragmatist would have pointed out at once, of course, the utter absurdity of the distinction, as if there were any fact apart from its presentation, and as if all presentation did not involve the personal equation of opinion. However, they went on some time suppressing and doctoring what they called' news, ' and merely conniving at mob-violence for the suppression of inconvenient opinions.

"This loose sham-voluntarism lasted for several years before it was recognised how essential a war service it was to drill the whole intellectual and spiritual forces of the nation into complete harmony with the supreme purpose of a State at war. A joint conference of the leaders of the Churches, the Universities, and the Press, was the instrument by which the War Council was at last induced to sanction a complete scheme of intellectual conscription, the natural concomitant of military and industrial conscription, in that it placed the minds as well as the body of all persons under military discipline. Of course, in an informal sort of way, a good deal had already been done in our schools, universities, and churches to bring them into line with the purposes of a patriotic culture and a genuinely British Christianity. But much remained to be done, and I am vain enough to think that in the work Pragmatism has proved of inestimable value, by supplying the really fundamental conception without which even the most bellicose of Deans or the most abject Master of a College would have spent his patriotic effort to little purpose."

"And, pray, what is that conception?" I asked, perceiving that Paston was still labouring with undischarged information.

"Well," he went on, "it is the simple notion that truth is a raw material, infinitely malleable and adaptable to purposes of State. Once grasp that notion, and the full potentialities of our Psychological Laboratory will become clear. We begin by accepting the familiar distinction, true for me, false for you. This idea of the relativity and adaptability of knowledge is then generalised and applied in the processes of our laboratory, for producing out of the same raw material the separate truths which war requires for the home consumer, the Ally, the neutral, and the enemy. The crude fact is the same for all; everything depends upon the treatment.

"You would be surprised to learn how quickly it becomes a matter of laboratory routine. Here is the' stuff' and there the recipient mind upon which a given war-impression is to be made. Given the analysis of the recipient, it becomes merely a question of preparing and applying the requisite Alloy."

"Alloy!" I exclaimed. "Do you really mean that you deliberately falsify the facts?"

"Not at all," he replied warmly, "you do injustice to the delicacy of our art. It is our duty to compose the sort of news which it is good for the respective parties to receive, and to mould the sentiments and opinions it is good for them to hold. And then, when our expert taster says that we have got it just right, it is pumped into the news agencies and the other publicity machines."

"But this," I interjected, "surely goes beyond all accepted usages of censorship even in war-time."

"Censorship!" exclaimed Paston, "We have long discarded this foolish term, and the false stress it laid upon the inferior art of mere suppression. That work, of course, still has to be done. The public mind must not be allowed to be confused or depressed by information which, however accurate and even interesting, is not nutritious. The same applies to all sorts of opinion and discussion. You would be interested, in fact, though possibly a little shocked, by the elaboration of our Index."

"You mean," I said, "Pacifist and pro-German literature, and that sort of thing!"

"Well, no," he said, "I wasn't thinking of such obvious prohibitions. We have found it necessary to strike deeper at the roots of intellectual licentiousness. You will find on our forbidden list, therefore, such well-known but mischievous works as Milton's' Areopagitica,' Locke's' essay on 'Toleration,' and Mill's' Liberty.' Indeed, one of the members of our Board, the Dean of Brabourne, was anxious to proscribe the unexpurgated version of the New Testament, a good many copies of which are said still to be about. But the really important work in the department, as I have already intimated, falls to the Board of Intellectual Inventions. It is here that what I called the Alloys are prepared. The head of the office, my right-hand man, is a really tophole creative artist. You may, perhaps, remember him—Young Peters of Magdalen [1] —who used to send in little sketches to the' Pink'Un.' [2] After that he drifted on to the' Daily Mail,' where he made excellent practice for several years. In fact, Lord N., who is Head of our Advisory Committee, put him into this job. He is a perfect genius. Such a light hand for the pastry, and quite a miracle for sauces!"

[1] An Oxford college.
[2] *The Sporting Times*, a weekly newspaper devoted to sport, especially horse racing, was informally known as the Pink'Un because printed on pink paper.

"Aren't you," I said, "getting a little mixed in your metaphors? Just now it was alloys and chemistry, and now you seem to turn to cookery."

"Well, never mind," Paston rejoined, "chemistry or cookery; it's all one. The latter term reminds me that in the Board of

Inventions we have an admirably staffed sub-department for the production of statistics. A certain section of the public, you see, is always avid of exact measured information, and we have a clever little group of trained men from the School of Economics [1] to give them what they want. But I have dared to reserve for myself the most delicate and interesting of all the jobs."

[1] Apparently the London School of Economics and Political Science, commonly referred to as the London School of Economics, founded in 1895 by the Fabian Society, a socialist group.

"And what," I said, "may that be?"

"Why the manufacture of the Myth. Ah, I forgot; the vogue of Sorel and the Syndicalist idea [1] came just after your time. Well, to put it simply, the Myth is the mightiest of all inventions, the brazen image of a great spiritual achievement which will fire all men with enthusiasm and stimulate their utmost effort."

[1] Georges Sorel (1847 – 1922) was a French Marxist who promoted the syndicalist movement involving general strikes. He advocated the invention of "myths" to sway the masses.

"Yes," I said, "I think I understand; something big and false to buck them up."

"Well, not exactly," Paston replied, "the Myth cannot possibly be untrue, because you see' it works.' Indeed, it is supremely true."

"Well," I said, "and what is your particular Myth?"

"It is the mirage of a world Democracy rising instanter [1] from the fumes of the blood-soaked battlefield. Whenever the vision gets a little dim, which happens sometimes as the war drags on, I get some great phrase-maker of our statesmen to put in a few new bright touches, or sometimes a vigorous journalist will lend a hand. In one way or another, we have managed so far to keep the fine old Myth in excellent repair. You have no notion what a lot of war-spirit it can be made to yield. When occasionally things look very black, I set to work myself and put some new allurements into the substance of the Myth.

[1] Instanter: instantly.

"But I don't want to run on talking about my own special job when there are others doing such splendid work. Young Peters, for instance, has a man who is perfectly splendid with the Explosives."

"Explosives! Why, what do you mean?"

"What should I mean? Material war must, of course, have its close counter-parts in the war of ideas. In that little office the preparation of the intellectual bombs takes place. Whenever our expert observers report signs of a collapse in the war-spirit of the enemy, so that there seems a danger of a really serious peace offer, we hurl one of them across the ocean, a brand-new economic boycott, or a fresh territorial demand. From time to time we vary these explosives by quieter but not less damaging infectives, poison gases injected through the Press to pass through neutral sources into the mind of the enemy.

"I can't go into details here, of course, but you can imagine we are pretty busy, what with our intellectual and moral bombing of the enemy and our soporifics and our stimulants for the irritations and war-weariness at home.

"But there is one department of our work in which you will be particularly interested. The Universities have behaved like trumps. As soon as they shed their early scruples about' objective' facts and' absolute reality, ' they took to the preparation of war-truth like ducks to water. Really splendid service, for example, has been rendered by their Joint Committee for Historical Reconstruction, under the Chairmanship of Dr. Norman Flower whose famous monograph, ' How Blücher lost us Waterloo, ' [1] has struck the shrewdest blow yet given to Prussian military prestige, besides winning for its erudite author the Paris Academy medal,

'Pour la vraie vérité.' [2] I need hardly tell you that there is plenty of work to be done for our schools and colleges in rewriting History in the *entente* [3] spirit, so as to delete the fabulous French wars, and to put in its true light such episodes as that of Joan of Arc. But equally good service is done by them in the capacity of Disparagers."

[1] Of course the British won at Waterloo, and the timely arrival of the Prussian field army under Marshall Gebhard von Blücher helped them do it.

[2] "For the true truth."

[3] Agreement – that England and France had always agreed, that is, been allies. Joan of Arc, mentioned next, ended the English occupation of France, which history must be "reconstructed."

"What are' Disparagers?'" I interjected.

"Why, the' Committee for the Disparagement of German learning.' [1] They have already got out some extremely damaging literature. Young Lewis of Balliol's' Seven proofs of the non-existence of Immanuel Kant, ' which took the Lord Mond prize last year, [2] has been published in eighteen languages for neutral service. Other pamphlets of conspicuous merit are Hyndman's' Damnation of Karl Marx, ' and a lighter brochure by Lord Haldane, entitled' How I burnt my Spiritual Home.' The Anti-Hegel Society is now proposing as a subject for its next meeting, ' The futility of Helmholtz.' [3]

[1] The sequel mocks the "Oxford Pamphlets on the War" in which distinguished academics distorted history to make Germany and Germans look forever bad. (This according to *The Revised Orwell*, Jonathan Rose, ed.)

[2] Referring to Alfred Mond, a pro-war industrialist, though he had not yet been knighted when the above was written. His chemical company profited from the war around this time and he was a large stockholder in the armaments industry. After the war he was

active in the Zionist movement.

[3] The author's purpose is to list a number of German intellectual luminaries, but the only one worthy of being so described is Hermann von Helmholtz, the physicist and physiologist. Kant, though paying lip-service to intellectual freedom, advocated an epistemology and ethics that would lead to the opposite; Hegel explicitly worshipped the State; Karl Marx (an expatriate) promoted communism. J. B. S. Haldane and Henry Mayer Hyndman, both Marxists, are here whimsically presented as renouncing Marx.

"A fine patriotic send-off to the whole campaign, of course, was given by the ceremonial burning of the German books from the Bodleian [1] at the Martyrs' Memorial. Perhaps you will have read some account of it?"

[1] The Bodleian Library is the principle research library at Oxford University.

"No. Everything you tell me is quite new and a little bewildering to one brought up in the older school of truth. But tell me: you have apparently demolished German philosophy and German science, but have you managed to do anything about German music?"

"Ah! do you know that just there you have hit upon the most perplexing problem that has yet confronted our Disparagers. At first, they were quite helpless in the matter, and were disposed to experiment upon the silly method of changing names. But they soon realised that it would take a full generation to substitute effectively the name of Hankinson for Mendelssohn, or Stokes for Wagner, and so they gave it up. Then somebody came out with the subtler suggestion for hiring third-rate orchestras to do their very worst in the Albert Hall, Queen's Hall, and other popular resorts, with Beethoven, Brahms, and other Hun masters. This proposal was actually approved by the Board of Disparagement, and a considerable fund was raised with the assistance of the Musicians' Mutual Benefit Society. Then came a quite unforeseen hitch. The first performances were rehearsed with care and given with really murderous effect. At least such was the intention. Unfortunately, the more cultured musical public took the perverse fancy to treat the most excruciating passages as a novel and fascinating phase of what they termed futurist transvaluation; and so the Hun names that had been advertised for execration came to acquire a fresh lease of undeserved glory.

"But I must not bore you any further with our innumerable engagements and campaigns in the great War of Ideas."

"Nay," I replied; "far from boring me, you bring both interest and profit. For I seem to come a little nearer to finding the correct answer to Pilate's famous question." [1]

---

[1] According to a biblical account, after having been taken to the hall of judgement Jesus said to Pontius Pilate, Roman governor of Judæa, "... for this cause came I into the world, that I should bear witness unto the truth. Every one that is of the truth heareth my voice." Pilate replied (and there is no response to him in the biblical account) "What is truth?"

CHAPTER IV

D.O.R.A. [1]

[1] When this satire was written D.O.R.A. was an acronym commonly used for the Defence of the Realm Act, passed at the beginning of the war, which empowered the government to do practically anything so long as the government deemed it necessary to the war effort. This title is the only place in the satire where initials are used for Dora, a personification and extrapolation of the D.O.R.A.'s power.

I FOUND Roxburgh of the Home Office[1] quite ecstatic about Dora. "I confess," he said, "that, when she first came to us, I didn't think she would be equal to the work. But when we'd fed her up with Orders in Council and two or three Amending Acts, she turned out a perfect treasure. Why, she can turn her hand to almost anything. She looks after the correspondence, gets rid of all sorts of inconvenient people, sees that the lights are turned down, tells us how much bread, sugar, meat, and coal we may have, shuts our public-houses, [2] and does all sorts of other philanthropic work.

[1] The English government office that supervises passports and immigration.

[2] Pubs: small restaurants that serve sandwiches and beer. After passage of the D.O.R.A. in 1914 eventually pub hours were licensed, and beer was watered down and taxed a penny per extra pint.
Then the State Management Scheme (1916) nationalized

39

breweries and pubs in areas of Britain where armaments were manufactured.

"And yet, would you believe it? At first Dora was not really liked. People actually complained that she was interfering, though it was entirely for their own good. They said they didn't like her reading their private letters and licking the envelopes; they didn't like her listening to their talk on the telephone, and they said that sticking people in prison without telling them what for wasn't playing the game."

"But surely she didn't do that!" I remarked.

"Of course she did nothing of the sort. This is a free country, and when anyone is charged with committing an offence he is entitled to be tried by his peers in public court, according to the law of the land. It follows, of course, that when a person is not charged with an offence, he has no claim to such a trial."

"Then why did they complain if Dora didn't do it?"

"Well, you see, it's this way. There were troublesome people knocking about whom Dora thought oughtn't to be left at large. Some of them were suspected of intending to do something calculated to interfere with military discipline, others of speaking disrespectfully of the Government, or even of saying spiteful things about Dora and her' carryings on.' Then, again, others were guilty of a thing called' enemy associations.'"

"And what," I interposed, "does that exactly mean?"

"Why, don't you understand?" Roxburgh replied, "the conspicuous merit of the term depends upon its not meaning anything *exactly*. It is really one of Dora's masterstrokes in semi-legal linguistics. You see it can cover everything, from the possession of a German dictionary to plotting to deliver Woolwich Arsenal to the Germans. And the best of it is that since it isn't an offence against the law, no charge can be brought, and so no evidence is required, no legal trial follows, no cross-examination or other defence, and, above all, no publicity."

"And therefore, I suppose, no imprisonment, no punishment!"

"Certainly not," was his reply. "Persons against whom such reasonable suspicion lies may be' deported' from their home and kept in' detention,' but they are never subjected to imprisonment."

"And where are they kept?" I asked.

"Why, usually in buildings otherwise employed for persons under legal sentence, but in this case described as' places of detention.'"

"But does it really matter what they are called?" I broke in.

"Why, you surprise me," said Roxburgh, "of course it matters everything. It would never do for a nation like ours to stain its glorious traditions of liberty and justice by imprisoning people without trial."

"Of course it wouldn't," I replied. "Pardon the clumsiness of my suggestion. But there is one other word you used on which I should be glad to have some light. You spoke of' reasonable suspicion.' And who decides whether the grounds of suspicion are reasonable or not?"

"Why, Dora, of course, and the impartial persons she appoints to look after her interests. These important matters cannot be left to the hazard of conflicting counsel, and the eccentricities of jurors. But as for grounds or reasons, they are strictly out of place. For, since you only suspect in cases when you cannot prove, the demand for evidence becomes irrelevant as well as inconvenient.

"I may tell you that one of the most valuable achievements of this war for liberty has been the liberation of the nation from the network of juridical and constitutional niceties in which she was in danger of being strangled. A free nation requires a free Government—that is a Government free to make and to unmake its laws and constitution as it goes along."

"And who are the persons that actually exercise this freedom? For in the last resort it is always persons who do things. Even Dora, I gather, doesn't do everything off her own bat?"

"Indeed, she does not. She frequently employs to carry out her orders what, with her dry humour, she describes as 'the competent military authority.' But the Privy Council [1] is also of great help to her, and even the Legislature chips in occasionally."

[1] A body of advisors to the British Sovereign (King or Queen).

"Yes; but that doesn't quite answer my question. These are machinery; for you don't suggest that Parliament or Privy Council acts *proprio motu*. [1] Who, then, are the persons that move them?"

[1] On its own initiative.

"Well, I suppose that in the last resort it is the members of the Government—I mean of the Cabinet, this is to say of the War Cabinet."

"And who," I asked, "appointed the War Cabinet, and conferred upon it this freedom?"

"Forgive my apparent rudeness," he replied, "but you are evidently out of touch with the spirit of our times, or you wouldn't ask such a question. The War Cabinet could only come into existence in one way, by virtue of that power of self-determination which is the essence of true freedom."

"And what," I said, "about the rights of the electorate—the representative principle, and all that?"

"Oh! the representative principle stands exactly where it did, and so do the other democratic principles. As principles they are quite innocuous, even praiseworthy, so long as they don't get themselves entangled with the practices of government. Indeed, it is essential to the smooth working of the new Plan that the people shall think and feel themselves' associated with' the Government. For we know they like to think that they are' doing it.' Like all children, you know! For from the standpoint of Real Politics democracy is a children's game. They have their children's parties, with lovely caucuses, mottoes, songs, and badges, electoral sports, and famous games of follow-my-leader."

"But surely," I said, "when they do get into Parliament they are liable to use the powers they find there—to' get entangled with the practices of government, ' as you put it."

"This doesn't really happen," he replied, "for the powers they find there are not real powers. They find plenty of pleasant enough recreations, excellent theatricals are arranged for them, house matches, paper-chases, cross-questions and crooked answers, and what not. There is plenty of fencing with buttoned foils and bodyguards, plenty of shouting and horse-play. But all the really dangerous tools and weapons have been put out of sight. Their noisy play has no real significance, and stops at once when they hear the master's voice. Nobody knows better than we officials how Government is really run, and just where the connections have been severed between the so-called will of the people and the operative powers of State. But, of course, it is our business not to tell."

Here I could restrain myself no longer. "Why, Roxburgh," I exclaimed, "your story is most disconcerting to one like myself, brought up on the old Liberal traditions. [1] The Parliament that you describe is not a Parliament of British Freemen—it is a Diet of Worms. [2] They cannot be so abject as you pretend. And even a worm—"

[1] Liberal in the old sense of liberty.
[2] A meeting of the legislature (Diet) of the Holy Roman Empire at Worms, Germany, in 1521, at which Martin Luther defended his criticisms of the Church. The Diet eventually issued the Edict of Worms, which made Luther an outlaw and banned his heretical books.

But Roxburgh broke in with his derisive laugh. "Oh, yes, at first they squirmed and wriggled, but we soon got them past the turning-point. The really troublesome ones were' taken over' by the Government, lucrative or honourable jobs were found for them. Dora put lots of them in what she called' Controls.' And so the wicked ceased from troubling."

"And the weary?" [1]

[1] Job laments: "In the world of the dead the wicked and the weary rest without a worry. Why does God let me live?"

"Oh, the obedient majority stood at rest, and took every dose of nasty medicine given them with obsequious gratitude. I tell you, my boy, it was at times a really pitiable spectacle to see a gathering of respectable old gentlemen reduced to such a pulp. I felt, sometimes, a sort of shame at helping to impose upon such helpless innocence. But there was nothing else to be done. The safety of the country and the continuance of the war were paramount considerations. It would have been wanton cruelty to saddle such a gathering with any real responsibility, or to entrust it with any real initiative. Anyhow, they didn't want these things: they were only too thankful to be told what they were to do, what laws to pass, and what money to vote. Recognising this, the War Cabinet decided to let Parliament have its way, and, however reluctantly, relieved it of the work it was no longer disposed to undertake. Moreover, it was a duty which they saw England expected of them. Besides, Dora, as you see, ever bright and resourceful, relieves them of most of their domestic duties. She and her two sisters-in-law, the one that looks after soldiers and the other that works in munitions, between them do nearly everything that is wanted to keep the country quiet and busy, and to tell all people what to do."

"But," I interrupted, "does everybody like to be told what to do?"

"They didn't at first, as I told you. They got quite angry with Dora when she started interfering with their home life, their diet, their free ways of talking, their treating of their mates, and their claim to choose for themselves the work they were to do. But their irritation soon settled down, and, now they have got used to her ways she is quite popular. You see it relieves them of the intolerable effort of thinking and deciding for themselves."

"But," I interjected, "I had always been brought up to regard this effort as the very pulse of British freedom."

"Well, you know," said Roxburgh, "speaking strictly among ourselves, when we first took on Dora and her sisters, all of us were subject to the same delusion—how that Britons stood for personal freedom, every man to be the arbiter of his own fate, and for something called civil liberty, the right to have a voice in making the laws one was called on to obey, the consent of the governed, and all that sort of thing. Do you know that it took us at least four years to discover that all this was nothing but the rhetoric of sentimental self-esteem—that it had nothing behind it."

"No!" said I, "you don't tell me so."

"Yes," he drove on, "it was this delusion that explains the ridiculous timidity of Dora's first advances, and all the stupid fumbling of our steps towards military and industrial conscription. You see, we were always pulling ourselves up to think, ' How much will they stand?' When we began numbering the people, we thought we had to conceal what it was all for. We didn't succeed, of course, for we were then novices in the art of war-truth; but it didn't matter. Then we lost two good years before we got full military service—and several more before we dared put industry on a sound compulsory footing. All this compromising, temporizing, and needless mendacity were due to the single error about British freedom."

"I am afraid that I don't even now quite grasp your meaning."

"I mean that it took us all these years to make the great discovery about the limit of governmental interference. Some put it at this point, others at that. Even long after the nation had taken military compulsion like a lamb, there still came up the big' Beer Bluff'—let not the Government tamper with the holy Cup!—the' Right-to-Strike Bluff'—British workmen would never give it up!—and several other Bluffs all based upon the superstition that there was a limit. There is no finer illustration of the power of words. Here was a Government, with all the necessary Prussian absoluteness in its hands if it knew it, held up in the performance of its most vital duties for years, just because it took for earnest the rhetoric of British liberty! At last, experience brought home to us the surprising truth, that there was no limit."

"And how," I asked, "did this discovery dawn upon you?"

"Well," said he, "some of us began to suspect it long before we had any clear assurance of it, and we waited for the tide of politics to throw up a really crucial test.

"What was it? Why, what do you think?—the appointment of Sir Edward Carson to the War Cabinet. [1] It was recognised by all of us that if the nation would take that stroke lying down they would take anything. And when we saw it raised not a ripple of effective protest, we knew that the country was ours and that we could give Dora her head. And experience has shown we judged aright, that Britons either didn't know what they meant by' liberty' or didn't care. And it was all one to Dora and us."

[1] Edward Carson, lawyer and statesman, helped remove H. H. Asquith as Prime Minister in 1916 and install Lloyd George. During the war he served as Attorney General, then First Lord of the Admiralty and in the War Cabinet. (Terence Rattigan's play *The Winslow Boy* is based on the Archer-Shee case of 1910 in which Carson was defendant's counsel.)

"And you really mean to tell me that you find no bottom to the popular servility, just as Paston claims to find no bottom to the popular credulity?"

"Servility! Credulity! You choose harsh terms, my friend, to describe what we have all agreed to call patriotic submission to our country's needs. And, after all, we do the thing quite handsomely, preserving the graces and amenities of the old political order. Just as we still keep up the forms of Parliamentary procedure, even to the ludicrous degree of voting money [1] that has been long ago been expended, so our public men still go about with serious faces consulting and conciliating public opinion and pretending to give their grave attention to the voice of a free electorate—an electorate just generously extended to the full figure of democracy. [2] You see it doesn't matter how many have votes, nor who they are, nor how they use them, now that we know we have the levers of real government firmly in our hands.

[1] To vote money is to determine a tax levy.
[2] A reference to granting women suffrage, anticipated when this was written and which actually occurred January 1918 with passage of the Reform Bill.

"We don't, of course, talk like this *coram populo*. [1] But plain words are all right between you and me. Now all this fuss about popular campaigns to win the wholehearted support of the democracy is quite unnecessary and a little farcical. They might just as well leave the whole business to us and Dora. For Dora can do anything she likes with them. There are now no discontents because there are no agitators. She has seen to that. If occasionally some wrinkle or crease appears in the smooth surface of public opinion, Dora just passes an iron firmly over it and it disappears. Why the People is now so tame, it comes and feeds out of Dora's hand. I mean what I say. There isn't a week passes but some well-signed memorial or petition comes up, begging for more regulations, or reporting the discovery of some little surviving liberty that needs stamping out. The incomparable Dora, who gives us all our weighted and diluted bread, reads our letters, curbs our unruly tongues, checks our comings and our goings, and keeps us from bad company! However, I must not let myself run on in rhapsody."

[1] *coram populo*: in the presence of the public.

"But," I broke in, "what about liberty and making the world

safe for democracy? [1] Is there no loss of liberty in the doings of Dora?"

[1] Evidently "making the world safe for democracy" was a common phrase in England at this time. It had become so over the ocean. On April 2, 1917, after about two and a half years of the war in Europe, American president Woodrow Wilson, though he had campaigned for re-election on the slogan "he kept us out of the war," gave a speech before a joint session of Congress asking for a declaration of war against Germany in order that the world "be made safe for democracy."

"Not at all," was Roxburgh's answer. "There is really just as much liberty as ever—only it is concentrated at the top. It is, as the poet sang: 'Of old sat Freedom on the heights' :

"'There in her place she did rejoice,
  elf gather'd in her prophet mind,
And fragments of her mighty voice
  Came rolling down the wind.'[1]

"That is our Dora launching her Controls, her Prohibitions, and her Permits. And in her service there is perfect freedom."

[1] The second stanza of Alfred Lord Tennyson's poem "Of Old Sat Freedom," slightly misquoted, composed in the early 1830s and first published in 1842.

CHAPTER V

THE MILITARY SERVICE (FEMALES) ACT

I WAS not a little curious to learn how women and the woman's movement had fared under the rules of war. For when I went out four years ago, the war-spirit had seized the women of all classes, and was hurrying them into munitions and other war-work, and some of the most renowned Suffragists were leading the Never-Endians. So I lost no time in looking up Martin, who had been my fellow-curate at St. Aloysius, and a mighty man of valor among the Church Suffragists.

I found him, as ever, abounding in enthusiasm for the cause and with the old exuberance of language. The great achievement of the Suffrage had, he explained, brought women back, almost with a jerk, to what he called "the primal verities."

"The life of the Home? The voice that breathed?" [1] I interjected.

[1] The beginning words of a wedding hymn: "The voice that breathed o'er Eden."

"Yes," he replied; but with a difference. The voice that breathed over Eden now blows hot and strong, as you shall hear. But it is no mere return to the Victorian home. The home is now firmly harnessed to the State, and finds its higher meaning in that service."

I don't quite follow," I broke in; "do you mean that the State 'controls' the home, and that an Englishman's house is no longer his castle?"

"Oh, no; it is more than ever his castle, for it is armed to meet

49

the enemy at the gate. You will remember the conflict that was always coming up between those who were interested primarily in securing home-rule for women, the right to marriage and children, payment for motherhood and housekeeping, with facilities for getting rid of husbands who didn't suit, and those who were for giving marriage and the family the go-by and inciting women to realise their potentialities in the larger fields of politics and business."

"Yes," I replied; "I remember how thick the air was with the recriminating cries of' free love, " race suicide, ' and the rest, and how embarrassing it all was for liberal clerics like ourselves, who saw the importance of the Church not alienating the advanced women of either camp."

"Well," said Martin, "the war with its plain lesson of reconcilement was most opportune."

"The lesson," I said, "may be plain to you, but it is not to me. How could war settle such a deep-rooted antagonism?"

"Why, simply enough. By enforcing the supremacy of a single obligation. You see, so long as the franchise issue blocked the way, the true relation of women to the State was obscure. Had the vote been won in peace time, it might have remained obscure. But the sudden bestowal of full citizenship in war-time made everything clear as day. Women were now invested with the full rights and obligations of citizenship at the moment when the nature of their obligation was most patent. For young men we saw that obligation take the shape of fighting for their country. For old folk, the supreme sacrifice was similarly ordained. On women of marriageable age the duty obviously devolved to repair the wastage of the war. This is pre-eminently women's war-work. For were it left undone, the war with all its liberating mission, would speedily collapse. A few more years would plunge the world into peace for sheer lack of the fighting material. It is for woman to avert such an unspeakable calamity."

"This," I interrupted Martin, "is very interesting. But tell me, do all the women see it in this light? Are they all willing to engage in repairing war-wastage? Some women, surely, don't want to marry and have families?"

"No doubt," said Martin, "but what of that? Some young men don't want to fight. Some old folk don't want to be cremated. But the stern logic of war, with its frightfulness, is not to be denied. Women cannot any more than men escape from the rightful demand of the State upon their services. I don't mind confessing that it has proved uncommonly difficult to drive home the imperativeness of this call upon some women. In fact, at first it was necessary to walk very delicately in the matter, for fear of forcing the feminist movement into the arms of the No-Maternity Fellowship."

"And how did you proceed?"

"Oh! we took the same sloping, zigzag road which served for getting the soldiers, the aged people, and the workers. By the usual methods of "inducement, stimulus, or pressure," we got hold of a good number of militant suffragists and put them on the patriotic appeal job. We placarded the walls with diagrams showing the inadequacy of the present low birth-rate to keep the war going for more than twenty years. Then there was the famous picture of the boy-baby, entitled' Watch him grow'—' In one year he will be the eighteenth of a soldier, in two years'—and so forth. And every wall rang out with the challenging appeal:' Mother, what did *you* do in the Great War?' [1]

[1] This mocks a recruiting poster of 1915 depicting a grim looking man sitting in a sofa chair, a boy playing with toy soldiers on the floor and a little girl on his knee saying something. The caption reads *"Daddy, What did YOU do in the Great War?"*

In the essay "My Country Right or Left" (1940) George Orwell wrote of the eventual reaction to the Great War and of "all the men who must have been lured into the army by just that poster and afterwards despised by their children for not being Conscientious Objectors."

"But the voluntary method was not really a success. We tried, of course, to stiffen up the moral appeal with material inducements, remissions of taxation, and even bonuses on parentage. But the trouble was that the problem of wastage is not entirely one of quantity. Quality also comes in. Now promiscuous bonuses on parentage were soon discovered to be a process of dysgenic selection .... In fact, it was the pressure of the eugenists upon this point that gradually forced us into the policy of the' Military Service (Females) Act, ' at present under discussion. But we didn't, of course, jump from voluntary into compulsory service in a single bound."

"I should think not. That would be most un-English. But what was your middle stage?"

"One which at first caused much heart-burning to good Churchmen in particular. It may be summarised by citing the two principal expedients employed. The first was a measure for the facilitation of conditional divorce."

"Ah; I remember the stir which the Report of the Divorce Commission raised before the war. But I confess it isn't obvious to me how the dissolution of marital unions helps towards solving your problem of raising the birth-rate."

"No; perhaps not. But I used the term' conditional divorce.' Now, the main conditions of the new Divorce Act were expressly designed to meet the difficulty you have in mind. In the first place, its operation was confined to cases where existing unions, lasting over a specified period, had not yielded the proper quota required to meet the estimated future needs of the military authority for the maintenance of our fighting forces."

"Still," I interrupted, "I cannot see how mere divorce—"

"No doubt," continued Martin; "it couldn't. But the second condition meets your point, for it restricts divorce cases where the claimant or claimants produce satisfactory proof of an agreed proposal for re-marriage with a properly certified person of' marriageable' age and character. This decree of divorce is only made absolute by the registration of the certificate of remarriage.

But though this induced a certain number of patriotic men to put away their ageing wives and to take on younger and more promising substitutes, it could not, of course, go very far towards meeting the requirement. For the essential difficulty lay in the wastage itself, that is to say, in the ever-growing gap in the numbers of marriageable men. Indeed, it was not long before military needs seemed to threaten the very institution of monogamy."

"You are most alarming, Martin," I exclaimed. "Surely the influence of the Church, even if it had to make concessions on divorce, was able to resist the degradation of polygamy?"

"Why, certainly," replied Martin hastily, "we have never budged upon essentials, though some concessions had here also to be made. In judging them, however, you must bear in mind that we are living under the Mosaic dispensation for the duration of the war."

"Well, what are the concessions?"

"Chiefly two. In the first place, we have been induced to sanction the practice of Concurrent Unions."

"And what may that mean? It reminds me of the old Police-court expression, ' sentences to run concurrently.'"

"Ah! I see you grasp the central meaning. Though some prefer to use the euphemism Cooperative Households, as presenting a more harmonious idea. Well, that is one expedient. Another is the adoption of leasehold or terminable marriages, though this, of course, overlaps with the facilities of divorce. But it was felt right that every marriageable woman should have a chance of serving her country, and that all minor considerations of pre-war custom or morality must yield place to this prime obligation. A most convincing exposition of the whole case was given by Father Compton in his sermon in the Abbey, in which he pointed out how in the patriarchal days both the concurrent union and the terminable marriage were recognised as Divine ordinances, designed to ensure the continuity of the family. 'And shall we do less,' continued the preacher with an eloquent gesture, 'for our

Fatherland, that larger patriarchy, the State, in whom on earth we live and move and have our being? Is it not the religious duty of all God-fearing men and women to raise families to the glory of the State?' It was an exceedingly serviceable utterance. For, coming just at the moment when the new amendment for including Short-leave in the Military Service Act was before the country, it silenced all serious criticism."

"But was there no real opposition?" I asked, "to these exceedingly drastic proposals?"

"Well, there was the so-called' One Man One Wife' party, but their propaganda was soon suppressed as pro-German pacifism, somewhat unfairly as it seemed to me. But the controversy has now died down, and all these expedients, so far as they have appeared to' make good, ' are now incorporated in the new Act."

And what are the main provisions of the Act?"

"Well, it sets up in every district a Tribunal of Women between the ages of forty-eight and sixty-five (the Aged service limit, as you will remember), and requires them to summon before them all women of marriageable age, not at present occupied in military service, who, when passed by the Advisory Committee of Eugenists, are enrolled in territorial companies to be called up for service as the competent military authority for the district may direct. Time is given to all duly certified women (now 'deemed' to be mothers) to qualify by voluntary contract, but if they fail to qualify within the prescribed period, they come within the compulsory powers of the Act.

"A drastic policy, you say. But the country must have soldiers enough to ensure the duration of the war. All private feelings and conveniences, it is felt, must bow before this paramount need. And how otherwise can the need be met? Besides, as historians point out, we cannot have the benefits of war without paying this price. Spartan military economy was based, as you remember, upon preferential rights for her fighting men. Athens, after the catastrophe of Syracuse, had resort to the same expedient; and, to come closer home, its recent adoption both in

Germany and Austria compels us to follow suit."

"You mean," I interjected, "that God will send in to the Kaiser the bill for any moral degradation that may ensue?"

"Well," said Martin, "you may put it that way if you like. I should prefer to say that the necessity of State washes out all guilty stains, consecrating each special sacrifice of personal feeling. But, of course, one can't expect so radical a policy to work quite smoothly. Indeed, among the military biologists a fierce Mendelian controversy is raging at the present time."

"Mendelians!" I exclaimed. "I thought they were absorbed in crossing strains of wheats and peas."

"Well! so they were when you left England. But like every other body of specialists they have been' taken over' by the Government and set to work at war-expedients. For some time they were innocently occupied in discovering the Mendelian characters which would yield a strain of bomb-proof nerve and another strain of war-truth brain tissue. But then a little group turned their energies upon sex determination and dominant and recessive characters involved in it. And then the fat was in the fire. For granted that by scientific feeding and judicious Mendelian selection you could control the proportion of male to female births, what is the desirable proportion in war-time? The problem, it appears, is not a simple one. ... Until we can get an agreed answer to this question, how can we ensure the indefinite duration of the war?"

"To my childlike intelligence," I said, "it would seem clear that the business of your Mendelians was to encourage the maximum proportion of males."

Martin smiled. "Yes, that is just the error that the novice in this thorny controversy naturally makes. If you were arranging for a comparatively short war, say, not longer than twenty or thirty years, of course, the more boys to-day the more soldiers eighteen years hence. But if you are guided by a wider military caution, you will take a longer range for the duration of this war, perhaps even keeping an eye upon the next war, and the next but one. Thus you will see that it is necessary to provide not only for a large crop of soldiers now, but for still larger crops to ripen later on—say, thirty or forty years hence. For this purpose it is as important to provide the mothers of the future armies as to provide soldiers for the existing war in its remoter stages."

"Ah, Martin," I exclaimed, "I see you are the same old militarist as ever."

"Yes," he replied, "and more convinced than ever. For war is not only the reconciler of class differences, it unites the sexes in co-operation for our supreme human purpose. Providence has assigned to man the *rôle* of the fighter, to women that of providing the material wherewith to fight. The voluntary rush of young women to the munition factory early in the war was indeed a gesture of instinctive symbolism, the unconscious feeling for their true mission. And," he added, with an ecstatic fervor, "that mission has an even wider sweep than I have indicated. It is woman's great privilege not merely to provide for this war, or the next war, but to provide for WAR. For without the pressure of population upon the means of livelihood, history teaches us that there could be no war, and that for lack of this bracing and cleansing struggle mankind would stagnate in comfortable and ignoble security. It is woman's part in the scheme of life to apply this pressure, in order to avert the peril and to secure that WAR shall not perish from the earth.[1] She has done her work gloriously throughout the ages, and, with the assistance of the Military Service Act, she will continue to do it."

[1] Mocking the caption "That Liberty Shall Not Perish From the Earth" of the Liberty Bond poster by Joseph Pennell (1860 – 1926).

"But," suddenly glancing at his watch, "I must tear myself away from this alluring conversation, though there is so much more to be said. For I have my Mothers' Meeting at seven, and I promised them a little talk on woman's duty in the home."

And so he left me, wondering what Euripides, the friend of woman, would have thought had he been there to hear. [1]

1 See Euripides' play *Medea*.

CHAPTER VI

WAR-BONDAGE

I HAD just seen some friends off at Euston, and was about to leave the station when my eye was caught by a battalion of men drawn up along a neighboring platform for entrainment. The spectacle of entraining soldiers had, of course, long been a familiar one, but there was something odd about the appearance of this lot that piqued my curiosity. They wore grey uniforms, carried no military accoutrement, and their general bearing was not that of drilled men. And yet they were evidently under discipline, for a few armed men were shepherding them, and a smartly dressed officer, who seemed to be in charge, was giving his final orders. As I drew near I recognised in this last my old school acquaintance, Hickson, who carried off all the prizes for mathematics in my time, but at Cambridge was switched off to Economics, where he won golden opinions for his skill in applying the calculus of the infinitesimal to the defence of Capitalism. Whenever we had met, as we sometimes did in the vacations, we had usually crossed swords on Labour questions, for I had always been something of a Socialist. But at the end of our arguments Hickson would escape into an attenuated atmosphere of abstraction, where I failed to follow him.

After I had accosted him, Hickson explained that he was now acting as an Inspector in the Labour Forces, and that the men waiting to entrain were a draft on their way to Crewe, which was the distributing centre of the North-Western command.

"And what becomes of them when they get to Crewe?" I asked.

"Oh! they are again medically examined, and are then sorted

58

out and grouped in squads for delivery at the various munition, mining, or other local centres where a labour shortage is reported."

"But," I interjected, "have they no say at all as to where they shall go and what they shall work at?"

"Why should they have?" was his reply. "How can they possibly know where they are most wanted and how their labour-power can be best applied? It requires an exceedingly elaborate study of the rising and falling curves of demand in the various localities and trades, and of the delicately graded' priorities' to know exactly where to put them. It isn't easy work, but it is uncommonly interesting."

"Well, Hickson," I said, "it is the last thing I should have expected of you, descending from your theoretical heights to the common pavement."

"Oh!" he replied, "I have really made no such descent. On the contrary, what you call the pavement has ascended to the heights of theory."

"There I don't follow you."

"Yet it is simple enough. You will recollect that for some time past the mathematical school had been making a bold bid for the control of economics."

"Yes, economic theory," I said, "but—"

"Don't," Hickson broke in, "be in too great a hurry. What the war has done is to place economic practice also in our hands, by making it conform to our abstract formulas. It has supplied what was really necessary to give practical validity to our' marginal' theory of values, viz. a supply of liquid labour." [1]

[1] In what follows we are reminded that in U.S. businesses the department charged with recruitment, once "Personnel," is today usually "Human Resources," as if people were like rocks and minerals.

"And what exactly may that mean?"

"Well," he replied, "you must be enough of a business man to know the term' liquid capital.'"

"Yes, of course," I said; "it is capital not yet appropriated to any particular use, or materialised in any special plant or material, but ready to flow into any channel that can profitably absorb it."

"Quite correct," he said. "Now, the trouble has always been that in the past labour has not been sufficiently liquid."

"You mean that the personal tastes and desires and the local attachments of the workers have impeded the fluidity of labour."

"Precisely. Labour has been a refractory material. In the first place, the worker insisted on having a will of his own, and deciding for himself what sort of work he would do. Then the trade unions raised artificial obstructions affecting quantity, quality, and methods of work and its remuneration. What was needed, not to put too fine a point upon it, was to remove this personal and collective will from labour, and to substitute the single governing will of the State motived [1] by the requirements of the military situation. Quite early in the war this need that the worker should place himself at the service of the State, on the same terms as the soldier, was apparent. Indeed, one or two of our Ministers made the damaging mistake of blurting out this truth before the atmosphere had been prepared, and the opposition of the trade unions sufficiently softened."

[1] Motivated.

"Yes, I remember the outcry five years ago when' forced labour' was first openly suggested. The big unions were up in arms at once, brandishing their menace of a general strike."

"Indeed," said Hickson; "this rash premature attempt at compulsion cost very dear. But it taught us our lesson."

"And what was that?"

"Why, that before we could proceed to make labour really liquid, we must take the trade union stiffening out."

"And how did you manage that?"

"Well, you see, early in the war the more patriotic trade union leaders went a good long way to meet us by suspension of their rules and usages, and especially by admitting the principle and practice of dilution."

"But," I interrupted, "only for the duration of the war!"

"Never mind that," he replied; "wait and see. Well, dilution, as the word implies, is itself a stage towards liquefaction, and the sort of labour leader who could be got to see the desirability of the one could be brought on to admit the necessity of going further. Indeed, it is fair to say that many of the leaders were from the first whole-hoggers, ready for the boundless submission of labour to be poured into whatever moulds the War Government might provide."

"And so by degrees the rank and file of the workers were won over?"

"Yes, won, or delivered, as you perhaps would call it, by their more pliable or liquid leaders."

"But, I suppose these leaders didn't serve the God-State for naught?"

"By no means. Why should they? They were much in request as officers in the new Labour Force. Indeed, long before a complete Forced Labour Scheme could safely be introduced, most of these men had done yeoman's service in helping to break the solidarity of labour through their British Workers' League. From broken solidarity to liquefaction is a simple process. Besides, our reformed school system played up marvellously well."

"How did that help?"

"Why, long before we got the crankiness of the trade unions thoroughly ironed out, the schools had been so improved that the whole adult youth of the nation poured out at eighteen either into the fighting or the labour forces, thoroughly disciplined and submissive to the needs of the State that owned them. This has been a mighty asset, for the knowledge that every year a larger proportion of labour passes in completely liquefied and' statified' makes the position of the refractory minority among the older men appear continually more hopeless.

"There is, of course, still some kicking even among the younger men. That is why you noticed the little knot of armed guards with the battalion we are shipping. They haven't all yet got into the spirit of the thing."

"So I should imagine. But, Hickson, I suppose this submissiveness, at first sight so surprising, is really a voluntary sacrifice 'for the duration of the war' ?"

"No doubt they think so. And so, to do them justice, does the Government. But any economist who has followed the evolution of modern industry must take a different and a larger view. Quite apart from the special emergency of war, liquid labour belongs to the ideal of the capitalist dispensation. [1] I am not, as you know, a religious man. But if I were, I declare that I should recognise in this war the finger of Providence."

[1] This and the sequel hopelessly garble the idea of capitalism, if by capitalism is meant laissez-faire capitalism where trade and government are separate, the government acting merely as an enforcer of last resort in a property dispute. Instead the author seems to use "capitalism" for anything to do with money, even and especially when business is *in league* with the government. His "capitalism" is actually the fascism he would oppose. On the other hand his "socialism" seems to be a perverse mixture of true (laissez-faire) capitalism and statism.

(It's interesting to note that Orwell, an avowed "democratic socialist," eventually gave unqualified praise to mid nineteenth century America – yet perversely continued to denounce "capitalism." Perhaps an excuse for the confusion of some English intellectuals can be found in European history: feudalism changed into capitalism, and they mistook the remnants of aristocracy – or just the fact that the former aristocrats started in the new dispensation with ill-gotten loot from the old – for capitalism.)

"Why, what on earth do you mean?"

"I have already answered you when I told you that liquid capital demanded liquid labour."

"But," I replied, "I am so dull that I don't understand your answer."

"Well, let me put it in this way. What is this capitalist system against which your Labour men and Socialists have been kicking? Is it the employer or manager of some factory, or mine, workshop, or office, who buys this labour and sets it to work up some sort of raw material with machinery and other plant? This employer or manager seldom owns this capital: for the most part he is himself the hired servant of some company or firm. Well, then, it may be said, you must look behind him for the enemy, who must be found in the persons that do supply the plant, machinery, and other real capital, the investors. But can these persons really be considered to exercise a responsible control over the capital which collectively they own? Most investors who furnish monetary capital do not know anything about the buildings and plant and materials it embodies itself in, or of the processes in which the labour is employed. Most of them are not even profiteers; they simply lend their money at a low market rate to the persons who direct a business. So, even here, you have not got down to the power-house of capitalism."

"Well, who are the real capitalists?"

"They are the men who control and direct the flow of liquid capital, those who gather in from innumerable channels the savings of a nation, and utilise them for fabricating the even huger volumes of credit which are poured through the financial system which they operate into the various moulds of concrete business.

"These men are the master craftsmen of the modern business world. It is their function to direct the streams of capital and labour. Capitalism has been steadily working up towards the final form of a free financial dynasty. By the time the war is ended, labour, like capital, will have been reduced to the frictionless fluid which is required. Capitalism will thus have reached its apex.

"That is what I mean by calling this a war of liberation. For it will not only have liberated capital from the chains of labour, but it will have lifted capital itself on to a higher plane of being, placing it in the hands of those who alone are qualified to use it properly."

"You mean, I suppose, your sublimated capitalist, the financier. But how does the war bring this about?"

"Why, with a beautiful simplicity of action. It substitutes for the countless forms of stocks and shares and mortgages and other certificates of ownership in many hands a single financial form, anchored in the safes of a few great Banks, Finance Houses, and Insurance Companies. These little groups of financiers already hold the mortgage deeds of Britain. Its lands and houses, mines and factories, ships and shops, belong to them. Such has been the secret achievement of the accumulating war-loans."

"But I thought countless thousands of ordinary men and women hold war-loans?"

"So they do, in name at least. But since all the later loans have been financed, partly by pledging earlier war scrip and all sorts of other securities with the banks, partly by bolder fabrication of bank credit, when the war ends, it will transpire that the war-financiers are the owners of all the property. For by that time the War Debt will have mounted up to a mortgage covering the whole estimated value of the national assets, and so the holders will virtually possess the country. Not only its capital, but its labour. For the labour of Britain will have to give up all the wealth it makes, beyond its necessary subsistence, to pay the interest."

"Do you really mean that the war has fastened this perpetual war-bondage upon labour when the war is over? Do you mean that when the saviours of their country return from their terrible ordeals, those that are left of them, they will be forced to spend the rest of their existence in grinding out profits for their creditors?"

"Now really, my dear Charteris, this sentimental rhetoric of yours is quite beside the point. Look at the process in a calmer and more philosophic light, and you will recognise its beneficent necessity. Force, here as elsewhere, is the midwife of reform: the stern logic of war has quickened the pace of capitalistic evolution, and has placed the supreme economic power in the hands most competent to use it."

"Yes," I burst out, "but to use it for what purpose? Your boasted financial dynasty seems to be nothing else than the return of serfdom. But, tell me, have you no fear lest these bondsmen may revolt?"

"Labour revolt! How can it? Can a liquid labour re-crystallise itself in separate obstructive wills? Still more, can it so stiffen itself as to present a solid front? But there is another reason why they will be impotent. They will not be allowed to know what has really happened. For the legend of financial ruin, universally believed, will continue to deceive them. The wail of investors over their depreciated securities will help to furnish a curtain of fiction behind which our real Capitalist smiles contented and secure. Nay, he will be in excellent favour as the peacemaker."

"Pray, how do you make out that *rôle*?"

"Quite simply. When capitalism has won, it will stop the war. For to go on further, and so to build up war-bonds beyond the safe limits of the real assets of the country, would be a lunatic proceeding."

"But you speak as if the financiers were the only persons whose voice counted. What about the Army? What about the Government? War policy surely rests with them."

"Oh! of course, the Army won't stop the war, for the pride of generalship and conquest is involved. And the politicians daren't, for to do so would be as much as their places, possibly their heads, were worth. But the financiers will bring the war to an end as soon as it has done its work."

"You mean its work of crushing German militarism?"

"Not at all. Its work of completing British bondage. Now that the war has performed its purifying mission in the organism of economics, as in that of politics, to continue it would be wanton cruelty as well as waste. Since a similar purification will have been taking place in Germany, the collapse of war will manifest itself as a natural necessity."

"But, exactly, how will capitalism stop the war?"

"Why, by starving it. By refusing to pour into its steel veins any more of the vital fluid from its sacred vessels."

"I see," said I. "But there is just one further question I should like to put to you, Hickson. At the beginning of our talk you spoke of labour as subject to' the single governing will of the State.' But now it would appear that the governing will is really that of a financial class."

Hickson hesitated just a moment, and then replied, "There is no real inconsistency. The State, you see, delegates its authority to various Controls. And just as it has appointed great mining and shipping experts to rule those industries, great grocers and millers to regulate our bread and tea supplies, what is more natural and proper than that it should assign to financial experts the province of national finance, with its super-control over all industrial processes?"

"But this financial domination you have described as permanent. And did you not represent its members as themselves reaping the profits of war-bondage?"

"Well, what of that?" rejoined Hickson. "The financier serves the State as the expert controller of liquid capital and labour, and, as a labourer in this fruitful field, is worthy of his hire."

"Even if his hire is the blood-money [1] of the nation?" was my parting comment.

---

[1] Here, money obtained at the cost of another's life.

CHAPTER VII

WAR AIMS

THE more I moved about and talked with people, the more it was borne home to me that the key to these bewildering transformations which were imputed to the war must be sought in the mind or guiding purpose of the nation. But how to discover that purpose? Reading of the current press, its books and newspapers, only filled me with discordant impressions, while intimate conversation with the persons I thought I knew best led to fresh bewilderment. For the gentlest-mannered people I had known boiled up into an almost speechless indignation when I tried to probe them about the purpose of the war, and hinted that I was little better than a pro-German for putting such questions. Indeed, I was almost led to abandon this inquiry, when I came across the quotation from Clausewitz[1] that "War is an act of policy." The word "policy" struck me, and I thought, "Well, after all, perhaps it is to the politicians I should turn for light and guidance."

[1] Carl von Clausewitz, a 19th century Prussian military theorist.

Roxburgh, to whom I applied for help, referred me with confidence to two volumes of War-Aim Documents and Speeches (1914-1920), in which, he said, I should find all the authoritative utterances from the early speeches of Mr. Asquith and Lord Grey [1] to those of Sir Horatio Bottomley and Dame Pankhurst.[2] I should also consult the similar collection of German documents

67

so as to comprehend the interplay of conflicting purposes. Everything would then, he said, become as clear as day. Meeting me a fortnight later, he asked me how I was getting on. I told him I had made a pretty thorough examination of the documents, but found my mind still held up on the threshold of understanding by what I feared would seem to him a childish difficulty.

[1] England declared war on Germany under Prime Minister Herbert Henry Asquith and Foreign Secretary Edward Grey.

[2] As noted in a footnote to Part I, Horatio Bottomley was a former swindler and later journalist and politician who promoted the war. Christabel Harriette Pankhurst was a suffragette who in 1914 declared a suffrage truce and began promoting the war. At the time this satire was written she did not yet possess the Dame title.

"What is it?" he inquired.

"Well!" said I, "I have read several thousands of pages about War-Aims without being able to discover what the writers and speakers mean by a War-Aim."

"I don't understand your difficulty. Surely our speeches and replies to Germany have made it evident that our aims are the crushing of Prussian militarism, the liberation of subject nationalities, the restoration of conquered territories, the enthronement of public law in Europe, and making the world safe for democracy."

"These," I replied, "are no doubt splendid aspirations, but can they be described, in a proper sense, as war-aims? Let me try and put my difficulty. In shooting, the aim of the shooter is the target, the bird, or other object he tries to hit. It is not the healthiness or interest of the sport, the sort of weapon that he uses, the prize he hopes to get as winner, or the personal prestige, though all these things no doubt count in the shooting. So in these pronouncements of War-Aims, I hoped to find definite, consistent statements of the actual objects to which the fighting was directed. Now, with the single exception, upon our side, of the restoration of Belgium, I find no such statement anywhere. Some of the so-called aims are quite indefinite, others appear to expand and to collapse with every change of war fortunes, others cannot be called aims at all. I find no fixed target anywhere."

"You are pretty sweeping in your criticism," said Roxburgh.

"Well," said I, "I have a mind that wants to understand, and I confess the prevailing mental and emotional atmosphere seems to me one in which people not merely do not want to understand, but in which they want not to understand, because they instinctively recognise that even to attempt to understand interferes with the free flow of passion. But may I explain my difficulty with some illustrations, if you have time to spare?"

"Certainly," said Roxburgh; "go ahead."

"Well, I've taken all the professing statements of War-Aims in your two volumes, and as a preliminary process subjected them to a quantitative analysis. I give you the results. Twenty-eight per cent., all the opening passages, are given to origins, the responsibility of the enemy for planning and precipitating the war. Forty per cent., all the next passages, are devoted to exposing with examples the lawlessness and calculated barbarity with which the enemy has conducted the war. Now, neither of these portions has the slightest relevance to War-Aims. For origins are not aims, and methods of conducting war are not aims. Of the rest, twelve per cent. do affect to deal with war-aims, while the last twenty are best described as the rhetoric' Never again.'"

"But," said Roxburgh, "granted that your statement is correct, are you not pushing your quantitative analysis too far? After all, allowance must be made for the language and methods of diplomacy. You can't expect statesmen to present their aims like the items of an ordinary butcher's bill."

"Indeed, I don't. But why pretend to send in an account at all, if you must mix up, omit, or so misdescribe the items as to make them unintelligible?"

"Ah! Charteris," he replied, "I am afraid your long absence from England has put you somewhat out of sympathy with our national genius for muddling through. May I suggest that perhaps what you call' mixing up' may be an indispensable preliminary to that process? But here's a man far better qualified than I am to satisfy your curiosity. You probably know Poynton. He is actually a member of the War-Aims Committee. I say, Poynton, here is Charteris complaining that he can't find any up-to-date, explicit, and intelligible statement of the objects of the war!"

"Explicit and intelligible statement!" exclaimed Poynton. "Good Heavens! I should hope not. Why, the whole effort of our Committee is devoted to baulking the curiosity of people who are not satisfied to see the show, but want to go behind and see how it is worked. These people have no notion how difficult and delicate a task it is for statesmen to keep a great war like this going. Why, if we were to issue weekly bulletins with the last up-to-date revised version of essential objects, we should have the whole war-fabric tumbling about our heads. It would not be possible upon such lines to keep going even a seven years' war, much less one of a really creditable duration."

"But why, may I ask, do you call yourselves a War-Aims Committee, conducting through the country a War-Aims Campaign, if you don't really intend to tell the people anything about it?"

"Oh! but we do. The people are quite satisfied with what you call our rhetorical stunts about the liberation of small peoples, the rescue of the world from German domination, making the world safe for democracy, and so forth. They bite their teeth into these glorious phrases, and so keep their noses out of the real business of the war. It is just fellows like you who try to butt in and spoil the game."

"The game, you call it! A pretty costly game, isn't it, to some of your fellow-countrymen! But, tell me, what is the game?"

"The game of war-aims? Well, it may perhaps be described as killing three birds with one stone. Only when you look upon war-aim pronouncements from this triple point of view, do all the obscurity, the reticence, the inconsistency, of which you complain, become intelligible."

"Well, what are these three birds, which, from your account, should themselves be the war-aims. What is it you are really after with your War-Aims Campaign?"

"Well, first and foremost, what we are after is national unity. And that bird is sometimes very shy. Why, if we were to make the explicit and intelligible statements you desire, the nation would be rent with controversy. Let me give one or two illustrations. Suppose we were to remove what you call the veil of rhetoric from the Paris Economic Resolutions [1] and reduce them to hard business, Free Trader and Protectionist would be at one another's throat. Or, if we brought down our committals to a League of Nations from its safe Utopian elevation to the ground of real and immediate politics, its utter inconsistency with the future both of Protection and Militarism would raise a howl of anger from both these quarters. Why wantonly disturb the public mind by telling them things they are perfectly contented not to know?"

[1] A complicated agreement among the Allies regarding trade among the Allies and between the Allies and the Central Powers.

"Yes," I interjected. "I suppose you are right in thinking that the price of unity is ignorance. But what about your other birds?"

"Well, the second is also unity, the unity of the Allies. A certain amount of reticence, or must one say even of illusion, belongs to the cement of every alliance. Were we to meet once a month and put down in plain black and white all the secret pledges and undertakings made under stress of circumstances, and all the particular claims, territorial and other, each Ally had pegged out, we should soon find ourselves in Queer Street, [1] to say nothing of the policy which these Russian idealists [2] still persist in pressing on us, the policy of' No Annexation.'" [3]

[1] To be in Queer Street is to be indebted to many people.
[2] Apparently referring to the Bolsheviks, who seized power in

Russia the month this installment of the satire was published.
[3] That no country would annex Russian territory.

"But I thought we'd accepted that long ago."

"So we have. But only, you must remember, as' a matter of principle, ' and with the qualifications which that expression carries to practical statesmen. If we had to do what you seem to require, reduce the principle to terms of concrete War-Aims, we should be at once in the soup."

"I don't understand you. Surely no territorial ambitions of ours brought us into the war. We shall get nothing out of it."

"Oh! I wasn't thinking of what we were to get. Though, of course, there are those German colonies and those pickings in Mesopotamia and in Palestine. It would be awkward to explain how we didn't want these things, but couldn't give them up now that Providence had put them under our trust; and how that the British Empire was one for the making of war, but five for the distribution of the loot. Neutrals simply can't be got to see the logic of the British Empire. We ought to have an Imperial Propaganda Campaign later on, with a really competent staff from the War-Truth Department, to drive home the meaning.

"However, as I said, I was thinking not of ourselves, but of the other Allies, all of whom have also pledged themselves to accept the principle of' No Annexation.'"

"Then, what's the difficulty?"

"Why, just this. It compels us to keep to that atmosphere of vague generalities of which you complain. For if we were to explain to all and sundry how that our interpretation of the principle excluded all cases of 're-annexation,' 'areas of legitimate aspiration,' 'historic rights,' 'defensive frontiers,' 'territorial adjustments,' not to mention 'colonies,' and that we only proposed the principle should be applied to the territory of enemy Powers, not only Russians, but other foolish sticklers for so-called consistency would gibe at us."

"You said you had three reasons for, shall we call it, reticence.

What is the third?"

"I wonder you should ask. In order not to inform the enemy."

"You mean that if the enemy learnt our demands, he would be better able to baffle their attainment?"

"No. Much worse than that. He might accept them, and then where would our war be?"

"You mean we might get all we asked for, and yet not what we want?"

"Well, that perhaps is one way of putting it."

"Let me try another. Perhaps all your war-aims manifestos, speeches, campaigns, are mere camouflage for your real aim, which is to win the war."

"Rather say to crush Prussian Militarism, and make the world safe—"

"Oh! spare me the rhetoric, please. We are not a public meeting. I have just one comment. Winning the war may be the way of attaining our war-aims, but it can hardly be itself a war-aim."

"Never mind your quibbling. It's the thing we're after. And the danger is lest we should get all your definite intelligible objects before we reach this goal. This, I don't mind telling you, is the final and all-sufficient reason for keeping the other war-aims dark. And Fritz[1] plays up nobly on his side. Why, his pronouncements are quite as unintelligible as ours. Take that splendid claim of his about' the freedom of the seas' and his play with' material securities.' As long as we can keep this sort of thing going, there is no serious peril of a premature peace."

[1] Fritz was the nickname for German soldiers or the personification of Germany. (The counterpart for Britain was Tommy.)

"But have there not been moments when he has seemed to want to let down' the game'?"

"Well, yes. There have been several anxious moments. But we are a patriotic people. Whenever Fritz shows signs of having had enough and puts out feelers, we have only to turn on our War-Truth hose to spray the public mind with a fresh current of well-preserved and authentic atrocities, and to instruct our Press to fit the suffixes 'intrigue' and 'trap' on to the Boche [1] proposals, and the awkward corner is successfully negotiated."

[1] Boche: disparaging term for German.

"I gather, then, that the sole aim of the War-Aims Committee is to keep the war-fires burning?"

"I must say, Charteris, that your jesting seems to me singularly ill-directed. Surely you will admit that our supreme consideration should be to ensure that the millions of precious lives we have spent shall not have been sacrificed in vain."

"And this you certainly ensure by pouring millions of more lives after them? But does it never occur to you that after all they may be sacrificed in vain, if the policy of conducting the war is such as to preclude the statement, and therefore probably the attainment, of any definite intelligible objects?"

"Charteris, you are incorrigible. But let me tell you, once for all, this talk about aims that are definite and intelligible is treasonable, for nothing is more likely to interfere with the unity of purpose in this nation and among the Allies for the conduct of the war."

"I apologise," said I; "I forgot for the moment that our one war-aim was the continuance of the war."

* * * * *

When Poynton left us, Roxburgh turned to me and asked whether I was satisfied. Instead of answering, I asked him whether he was still dabbling in astronomy during his spare time.

"Yes," he replied; "I do a little at it; but why do you ask?"

"Well," I answered; "I remember how you used to talk to me

about the possibility of human life in Mars and in some of the other planets or stars. Now as Poynton was talking, it came into my mind to ask you this question, 'Has it ever occurred to you as possible that this planet may be the lunatic asylum of the Universe?'"

CHAPTER VIII

THE NEW JERUSALEM [1]

[1] It might seem odd to find Jerusalem featured in a satire about World War I, but Zionism – the idea that all Jews should band together and go live in their own separate nation – thrived among some successful Jews in war industry and finance. Also it was at this time that the Ottoman Empire broke up and Britain carved out Israel and the surrounding area as its "Palestine Protectorate." Only six weeks before this installment's publication (mid December 1917) Arthur James Balfour ("Lord Balfour"), Britain's Foreign Secretary, wrote a brief letter to Walter Rothschild ("Lord Rothschild") for conveyance to the Zionist Federation. The letter stated that "His Majesty's Government view with favour the establishment in Palestine of a national home for the Jewish people, and will use their best endeavours to facilitate the achievement of this object ...." This letter became known as the Balfour Declaration.

The author of *1920* depicts Zionists as having bought all the available Holy Places in Jerusalem for the purpose of constructing pleasure resorts. The Bishop of Silchester, "the most pushing of those younger prelates who ... were taking the Church firmly in hand," is unhappy because the Church will not get to share in the exploitation of Jerusalem as had been agreed upon between the "Saloman-Schiff crowd" and the "pan-Christian Board of Works." IT was a stroke of luck for me that Roxburgh should have been appointed one of the Commissioners of the Palestine Protectorate just before I received my summons to return to my post in the

Chinese Inland Mission. For it helped me to realise a plan for some time vaguely floating in my mind, to break my journey at Port Said, put in a fortnight's travel through the Holy Land, perhaps reaching Jerusalem in time for the tail-end of the great pan-Christian Synod. [1] Roxburgh, of course, had at his disposal every facility of travel, and seemed glad of my company. We had an uneventful voyage, and, arriving at Jerusalem, found it in the possession of a cosmopolitan crowd collected from every corner of the earth. We put up at Lyons's new caravanserai, the "Cœur de Lion," fitted out with every convenience: swimming-baths, theatre, a Boots' Library, and a snappy little newspaper *The Prophet*. After dinner, we spied in the great Fumoir the robust figure of the Bishop of Silchester, the most pushing of those younger prelates who, favoured by the Old-Age Service Act, were taking the Church firmly in hand. Silchester I knew was filled with the spirit of scientific management, which he deemed as applicable to religion as to any other line of business.

[1] Synod – church council convened to decide an issue of doctrine, application of doctrine, or church administration.

Roxburgh, who knows everybody, introduced me, and we sat together smoking. We found him in a great state of indignation. It wasn't so much the Synod itself that was the trouble. He had recognised all along that the Unity of Christendom was an exceedingly delicate plant, needing the utmost care from Paul, Apollos, and the other gardeners. The warring sects and missions could hardly be expected to yield at once to the healing influence of a Pax Britannica which had fought its way so recently into the holy Citadel.

"Well, Bishop," said Roxburgh, "what is the real trouble? Possibly I may be able to be of some service."

"It's that Saloman-Schiff crowd," [1] replied the Bishop. "And after all that British Christianity has done and suffered for the restoration of their country! Besides, you know that I, at any rate, have always been insistent on giving the financiers a fair show."

[1] The original version published in *The Nation* reads "Guggenheim-Schiff." Daniel Guggenheim was a wealthy American heir who was an influential member of the National Security League (headed by J. P. Morgan) which promoted U.S. entry into the war. The cofounder and head of the National Security League was Solomon Stanwood Menken.

Jacob Schiff, another American (an immigrant from Germany), represented Rothschild financial interests. Both Schiff and Guggenheim profited from the war and generously financed the Zionist movement. Schiff had helped Woodrow Wilson get elected in 1912, and, according to the American businessman Benjamin Freedman, an associate of Schiff forced President Wilson to reverse his isolationist policy during his second term. Also, by giving monetary aid to Russian Jewry, including and especially the Bolsheviks, Schiff helped bring about the Russian Revolution, which began the month this satire began serialization.

"Well, what have they been up to?"

"Why, when actually pretending to bargain with the pan-Christian Board of Works on a share-and-share alike policy, they formed a private syndicate, sent out secret agents to deal with the sheikhs, and got options upon every one of the Holy Places not previously pre-empted—all with a view to a vast Development Scheme of their own."

"Yes," said Roxburgh, "that is playing it rather low down. But, after all, does it matter so very much? When you want money, you must go where money is."

"Does it matter, my dear sir! It matters everything. Why, what is to become of the great new hope of a Christianity consecrated by the blood of myriads of crusaders and radiating a holy spirit of atonement from the very field of Armageddon? Think of all the sacred memories handed over to the desecrating grip of Judaism. Of course, I didn't say all I felt before the Synod.

Everybody knows that I have always stood for compromise and accommodation."

"But, surely, Bishop, you were able to do a deal with the Jew Syndicate? For, after all, politics count, and Palestine remains a British Protectorate."

"Well, I tried bargaining. I offered them not only practically all the Old Testament values, but threw in one or two concessions to their scheme of a pleasure city; for instance, the 'joy' railway up the Mount of Olives, with the Casino at the top. But I struck a particularly tough streak of Hebrew obstinacy. And they kept bringing up one argument which I confess was rather awkward for our Board to meet."

"What was that?"

"Well, it was the dispensation voted by Convocation for what is popularly called 'the return of Moses.' I never liked this step. It ought to have been managed in another way. They kept throwing this in our teeth, insisting that we had given away what they readily termed 'the whole Christian show.' Of course, there's nothing in the argument, for when the war is over we shall soon become as Christian as ever. But it was a good debating point. I tried to turn it by carrying the conflict into the camp of finance, reminding them that the success of their developmental plans would, after all, depend upon the popularity of Jerusalem among the Christian peoples. I put it to them as business men. Were they not out for capitalising the goodwill of the Holy Places on a sound popular basis? How, then, could they dispense with Sir Henry Lunn [1] and the Y.M.C.A. tourists?"

[1] Henry Simpson Lunn (1859–1939). An ordained minister and physician who founded several travel companies featuring tours that combined a religious retreat with healthy activities such as winter sports.

"That seems a sound enough argument?"

"So I thought. But Meyer (the Hirsch-Goldstein man, you

know) made a rejoinder which was a little disconcerting and needs thinking over, when he insisted that after the war the Jews alone would have the money for expensive travel.

"It's a most serious situation. For the position of the Christian Churches in the West, as you know, is exceedingly precarious. Our necessary war concessions have been an easy target for superficial scepticism. Everything now depends on having in our hands the wonder-working glamour of Jerusalem. But everywhere they are trying to thwart us. For instance, there is that great historic Cinema of the Holy City. Do you know that, in the alleged interests of historic continuity, Glucksteins, who were to produce the films, are now insisting that the whole of 'the Jesus story' shall be presented from what they call the objective standpoint as an incident in Jewish history. An absolutely wrecking policy. I put the matter plainly to Saul Gluckstein himself. 'Speaking for the Christian Churches, where do we come in?' Unfortunately, they had got hold of some of the Palestine Exploration cranks, who put in a lot of nasty probing as to the historicity of several of the Holy Places."

"I suppose," I interjected, "there must be a certain amount of discordance between the religious and business interests?"

"Well," he replied, "it's not exactly that, though on the surface it may seem so. Take, for instance, the famous case of Bethesda which is before the mixed Tribunal. Here is a squabble between a group of Italian monks, strongly backed by the Vatican, seeking to exploit the waters for miraculous healing, and a syndicate of hard-headed Scotch doctors who, finding by analysis rich carbonic acid deposits, see in it an admirable substitute for Nauheim. [1] Why, the faction fight between the partisans of these two schemes became so serious that the Arab Guards had at one time to be called in. Quite like old times.

---

[1] Referring to the naturally carbonated water from a spring in Nauheim, Germany. The area was a popular retreat for taking what was called an "effervescent bath" or "carbonic acid bath."

"But the crucial example is the grand scheme for the restoration of the Temple. The financial operation is, of course, in the hands of the great international syndicate, who, while preserving the ancient plan and proportions of the building, propose immensely to increase its size and to plant round it a vast garden suburb of eligible villa residences, to be occupied by the officials of the international finance bureau. The scheme was hatched since I left England, and I do not profess to have a clear grasp of its meaning. Perhaps you, Roxburgh, can throw some light upon it?"

"Well, yes. I think I can," said Roxburgh. "For I have had several long talks about it with Abram Hart, who, you know, is the moving mind in it. His central thought is that of making the Temple symbolise the harmony between what he terms the two converging spiritual influences—finance and religion. They are the two modes in which Faith or Credit finds full expression.' So long,' he says, 'as they are kept apart, or even treated as rivals for the heart of man, conflicts will arise. Not until business is stripped of its materialistic husk and refined into a purely spiritual process can religion ever win its full dominion, playing freely through all those processes of life deemed "secular" according to the old false dualism.' Hart first approached the subject as a practical financier."

"Wasn't he the man who, early in the war, engineered the great copper corner?" I asked.

"Yes," said Roxburgh, "that's the man. But he had not then found illumination. It came, he says, as a flash to him that it was precisely this reconcilement that the Hebrew genius was in search of throughout history. Everywhere the Hebrew had shunned, by a sort of providential warning, the baser sorts of manual labour. His instinct was always for' value' and for those modes of commerce by which value was created without degrading toil. Such materials as he consented to handle as craftsman were those where crude matter played the smallest part, skill and cunning the largest. So everywhere he kept emerging as the dealer in the most abstract and general of all values, money; and money he persisted in refining into the spiritual and intellectual qualities of faith or confidence.

"Everywhere, so Hart contends, he has been misunderstood. For in all those processes of financial evolution, which have now culminated in the International Reserve Bank of Jerusalem, it was the religious prompting that was at work and refused to rest until the reconcilement was effected and the economic striving reached its spiritual goal.

"This great ultimate truth was to be symbolised by the ceremonial deposit of the Gold Reserve, upon which the whole fabric of world finance now rests, in the vaults of the Temple, the economic Holy of Holies. Such was the gist of his conversation with me."

"And I dare say," replied the Bishop, "that there's something in it. But surely it is carrying it a little far to propose that the ground floor, carrying the pillars of the Temple, shall form the premises of the Gold Standard Bank and the International Bourse with all its tapes and tickers. To set up once more the money-changers' tables is surely too much of a slap in the face for Christian tradition. Why, they would be wanting licenses to sell doves next, and what would then become of the duration of the war?"

Roxburgh here broke in: "But Hart insists that the whole money-changers' story rests on a vulgar misunderstanding of the rabbinical teaching that 'there is money in religion, and religion in money,' with its repudiation of the false dualism in the divine purpose. It sets in a new light, he contends, the doctrine of Atonement."

"But surely," I murmured, "no man can server two masters."

"Tut! Tut!" said the Bishop. "I don't deny that there is much to be said for Hart's policy of reconciliation. If I may express myself with due reverence, I have always regarded that strong antithesis of God and Mammon as somewhat needlessly overstressed, or, at least, unfortunately worded. The Church of England, at any rate, has never stood in the way of an accommodation, nor, it is fair to add, has any of the major Churches of Christendom. My criticism of Hart's policy is that it tends to give too conscious a prominence to a controversial issue. Let it remain an open philosophic question whether the relation between the two shall be of the nature of a complete' merger,' a balance of power, or a working arrangement modifiable to meet the needs of each country and each age. My mind inclines strongly to the last treatment, as more plastic and more conformable to the spirit of compromise. Our British genius is for letting incompatibles jog along together as best they can, keeping them from inconvenient encounters as far as possible, but not insisting that they shall embrace each other."

"Then you do not, Bishop," I slyly suggested, "yearn after the unity of a 'higher synthesis'?" [1]

[1] A reference to the third stage of Hegel's dialectic, an inexplicable process governing the production and combination of opposites.

"Well, no," he replied, frowning slightly; "a *modus vivendi* meets my inclination better."

"Isn't that usually called making the best of both worlds?" Roxburgh playfully interjected.

"Maybe, maybe," the Bishop replied, a little testily. "We are in this world after all; it is our duty to make the best of it."

"And take the best of it?" I ventured to put in.

"Ah, well," the Bishop smiled; "Providence has sometimes laid our lines in pleasant places. But we must always remember that the march of civilisation is justified by its mission.

"But talking about marches reminds me that you are just in time to witness the greatest of all the spectacular scenes in connection with the Restoration, which takes place to-morrow."

"And what is that?" I asked.

"Oh! the ceremonial return of the Chosen People to the City of Their Choice, followed by the solemn service of renunciation."

"And what," I asked, "do they renounce?"

"Two things, I understand; first their sojourn in the House of Bondage so long and so unwillingly endured."

"And do they," I inquired, "propose to leave their bonds behind?"

"Well, no," he said. "I gather they intend to lay them formally upon a temporary alter erected in the vestibule of the Temple, afterwards to be transferred to the vaults. One of the most interesting groups in the procession consists of representatives of the Transvaal Companies, who will with due solemn rites transfer the soul of the Rand, its share certificates, from Johannesburg to the New Jerusalem, thus completing the spiritual symbolism of the Golden City."

"But you said there were two acts of renunciation. What is the other?"

"The renunciation of the Gentile names which they were forced to bear in their unhappy exile."

"Forced to bear!" said I. "Why, I thought that—"

"Never mind that," broke in Roxburgh, rather rudely. "It will be a great day that sees every Montagu reverting to his proper Samuel, every Lowe and Lee and Law confessing Levi, and all the Monds, Eltzbachers, and Blumenfelts relinquishing their patriotic grip upn Britain in order to take up their citizenship here."

"Yes," replied the Bishop; "they will be sadly missed at first. But time will assuage our grief for this as for other losses. And besides, they will not be wholly lost to us. For we must not forget that Jerusalem is now a city of the British Empire, and possessing a 'peculiar people' it has a peculiar part to play under Providence in our Imperial purpose."

"I fear," said I , "that I don't quite understand what that sacred purpose is."

"My friend," he replied, "have you forgotten the words of the sweet Psalmist:' Jerusalem is built as a city that is at unity with itself'? It is assuredly designed that this spirit of unity, radiating from the holy capital, shall gradually fill the whole of our great Empire with its healing virtue. No," he continued, evidently recalling a fragment of his famous sermon on Alliance Sunday; "the age of miracles has not passed, nor may this spirit of unity be confined within the broad limits of the British Empire. I see a vision of our puisant Confederation drawing its free invigorating draughts of spiritual and financial power from the same unfailing fount—the New Jerusalem."

* * * * *

After the Bishop had retired I took a stroll down the Valley of Jehoshaphat?" [1] before turning in, and found myself humming in an undertone the tune of the famous hymn, "Jerusalem, the Golden."

[1] Joel 3:1-3: "I will gather together all the Gentiles, and will cause them to descend into the valley of Jehoshaphat, and there I will enter into judgment with them because of my people and of my heritage Israel, whom they scattered among the nations, and parted my land." (The Jubilee Bible)